redsine
issue eight, april 2002

EDITED BY
TRENT JAMIESON & GARRY NURRISH

REDSINE MAGAZINE • PO BOX 1287, TOOWONG, QLD 4066, AUSTRALIA • WWW.REDSINE.COM

REDSINE
a quarterly magazine of dark fantasy & horror

ISBN: 1-894815-01-7

Published by Prime Books, Inc.
P.O. Box 36503, Canton, OH 44735, USA
www.primebooks.net

Copyright © 2002 by Redsine Magazine.
All rights return to individual authors and artists upon publication.

Cover art copyright © 2002 by Garry Nurrish.
Artwork on pages 24, 55, 79 copyright © 2002 by Geoff Priest.
Artwork on page 107 copyright © 2002 by Mark Roberts.
Cover and interior design copyright © 2002 by Garry Nurrish.
Redsine logo copyright © 2002 by Geoff Priest.

No portion of this magazine may be reproduced by any means, mechanical, electronic, or otherwise, without first obtaining the permission of the individual authors and artists.

For more information, contact Redsine.

Redsine editors:
Garry Nurrish, Senior Editor - garry@redsine.com
Trent Jamieson, Fiction Editor - trent@redsine.com
Nick Gevers, Interviewer - nickgevers@redsine.com

REDSINE MAGAZINE
PO Box 1287, Toowong, QLD 4066, Australia
www.redsine.com

CONTENTS

5. DRAWER OF THE DARK:
An interview with Tim Powers

17. ELECKTRA DREAMS
Geoffrey Maloney

27. TRAPDOOR
Darrell Pitt

36. THE FACELESS MAN
Gene O'Neill

49. WITHIN TWILIGHT
Chris McMahon

57. LES AUTRES
Adam Browne

61. WAKE WHEN SOME VILE THING IS NEAR
Michael Kaufmann & Mark McLaughlin

81. THE WRONG STUFF
David McAlinden

88. ONE DAY AT A TIME
Hertzan Chimera & M. F. Korn

94. SPIRIT OF RAGE
Iain Darby

104. OCTOBER EYES
Alison L. R. Davies

109. MR OCTOBER
Jack Fisher

111. PAY PER VIEW
Jess Butcher

115. ROBIN HOOD'S NEW MOTHER
Rhys Hughes

130. BROTHERS OF PASSION
Michael Laimo

DRAWER OF THE DARK:
AN INTERVIEW WITH TIM POWERS
by Nick Gevers

INTRODUCTION

Tim Powers is probably America's most original contemporary literary fantasist, and by some reckonings the best of them all. Born in 1952, a close friend of Philip K. Dick in that SF magus's latter years, Powers began his career modestly but promisingly with two futuristic swashbucklers, *The Skies Discrowned* (later revised as *Forsake the Sky*) and *An Epitaph in Rust*, both published in Canada in 1976. His highly distinctive brand of fantasy—vastly complex, set in intensely realised locations, riddled with skeins of occult conspiracy, and featuring protagonists whose involvement with the supernatural follows a dark perverse logic chillingly threatening to body and soul—began to take definitive shape with *The Drawing of the Dark* (1979), a memorable vision of King Arthur reincarnated to save Vienna from the Turkish siege of 1529. Powers's most famous single novel, *The Anubis Gates* (1983), was one of its decade's most compelling adventure tales in any medium, taking a modern scholar of Romanticism back in time to his subject period, a pilgrimage entailing exchanges of bodies, visits to a fantasticated pre-Victorian London underworld, and confrontations with superbly depicted sorcerous evildoers; scarcely less vivid were *Dinner at Deviant's Palace* (1985), a retelling of the Orpheus and Eurydice myth against the background of a devastated future America, and *On Stranger*

Tides (1987), a fuliginous story of Blackbeard the pirate king and lunatic questings after immortality in 18th Century Florida.

After these triumphs, Powers began to write longer, perhaps more considered, but still hectically detailed and paced fantasies. *The Stress of Her Regard* (1989) is an astonishing take on possession, a secret history of inorganic life that explains in nightmarish terms the genius and the downfall of the great Romantic poets. Powers's huge Fisher King trilogy followed, made up of *Last Call* (1992), *Expiration Date* (1995), and *Earthquake Weather* (1997); accounts of magical influences and mythic resurrections on and around America's West Coast, these books insinuate opulent levels of strangeness beneath modern America's veil of normality, to bizarre and potently subversive effect. The mystical underbelly of the 20th Century is unveiled with especial virtuosity in *Declare* (2000), in which djinni and arcane rituals put a rather unaccustomed complexion on the Cold War; this is probably Powers's finest novel to date. His spare output of short stories was finally assembled in early 2001 in an impressive small press volume, *Night Moves*.

I interviewed Tim Powers by e-mail in October and November of 2001.

•

THE INTERVIEW

NG: Your novels are long, complex, charged with elaborate symbolism: a very consistent body of work. How would you sum up the Tim Powers Literary Aesthetic?

TP: Well, whatever it is, it's something I haven't deliberately constructed; it would be some sort of synthesis I've inadvertently put together from writers I've admired, I imagine. The things I think are important are . . . well, I think a writer needs to make the situation as believable as possible, plausible characters in very tangible and visible settings. The reader needs to forget that he's not actually in the presence of these characters, in these settings. I find any whiff of tongue-in-cheek fatal to this effect. And then of course the problems the characters are faced with have to be problems worth an intelligent person's concern! "I hope I don't die here" is one, certainly, but there are lots of others—"I hope I don't let everybody down, I hope I don't lose my mind/identity, I hope I'm not turning into someone I despise." And then I outline and plot obsessively, to try to set the characters up against these problems most dramatically. Maybe most of all, I want to give the reader a feeling of vertigo, dislocation, disorientation; ideally I'd like to give them the shivery, not altogether scary feeling of awe that Rudolf Otto and C. S. Lewis call the "numinous." As a reader, I treasure books that can do that—such as Lewis's *That Hideous Strength*, or Hope Mirrlees's *Lud-in-the-Mist*—and I'd really love to be able to do it too.

NG: Who then are your literary progenitors, obvious (Rafael Sabatini, etc.) and less obvious?

TP: In addition to Sabatini, I'd put up Robert E. Howard, John D. MacDonald, and Fritz Leiber—those are the writers I find I'm very aware of when I'm writing adventurous-type stuff. For the supernatural effects, I think I mostly lean on H. P. Lovecraft, C. S. Lewis, and Lewis's pal Charles Williams. And then for general style I imagine I bounce around among Kingsley Amis, Hunter Thompson and Tom Wolfe—which is a pretty wide range, now that I think of it! I just hope I manage to fit some original "Powers" in there, among all the strong influences!

NG: It's well known that you, James Blaylock, and K. W. Jeter constitute a literary affinity group, rooted in your common acquaintance with Philip K Dick. How has Dick's influence played out in your own writing? Are the three of you still conscious of being The Heirs Of Phil Dick?

TP: I think Dick was, for us, an example of how to be a writer, rather than of how to write. The thing is, he was a genius, and none of us are. In my own writing, I can see that I learned a lot from Dick about how to do characters, especially toiling, unglamorous characters; and of course Dick—like Lovecraft—invented a whole new brand of "scary" with his visions of crumbling realities, and I think I've used that perspective here and there. But we didn't really talk much about writing, when we all hung out together! Mostly he was a good friend and drinking companion.

NG: Your signature character, shared with James Blaylock, is the apocryphal 19th Century poet William Ashbless. How did this figure evolve, and how constant a presence is he in your fiction, early and recent?

TP: Blaylock and I invented Ashbless in our college days—about 1972—as a name under which to submit portentous-but-bogus poetry to the college newspaper. After that, he and I used the name for any crazed old poet we might happen to have appear in stories we were writing, and it seems there was a lot of call for that. When we began to get published, Ashbless was just part of our luggage! I don't know if Blaylock keeps on putting Ashbless in his stuff, but to me it's become something like a good-luck charm. I always mention Ashbless somehow—though lately I've begun using the Spanish version of the name, Ceniza-Bendiga.

NG: How influential is your Roman Catholic background on the moral and symbolic content of your books? Catholicism seems a particularly enriching basis for fantasy writers to work from . . .

TP: I don't know how much it influences my perspective, really—you seldom *think* about your basic perspective!—but I suppose it's made me put together protagonists who have to choose to do the difficult right thing, when really they'd rather not; and to make villains who are deliberately bad, not just helpless products of a bad environment. I guess it's in "free will and conscience" that the Catholic influence shows up in my writing, but of course you don't have to be Catholic to find those things important! And I suppose it has inevitably coloured my attitude toward the supernatural, which I write about a lot! Catholicism says that things like . . . oh, you know, ghosts, demons, vampires, genuine fortune-telling . . . are (A.) real, (B.) rare, and (C.) bad. So I think I've followed that simple formula in my fiction (a fantasist's version of Asimov's Three Rules of Robotics!). And I always see magic as damaging to its practitioners. I think I got that from C. S.

Lewis. I always postulate that it will work, but prolonged exposure to it will blunt and coarsen the practitioner, and even eventually whittle away IQ points.

NG: Your characters are often threatened with the imposition of identities not their own. To what do you attribute your pre-occupation with the alienation of the self?

TP: I guess it must be a thing I find particularly horrifying!—since I do, as you say, seem to use it a lot. I thought it was particularly awful in *Last Call*, when the real Betsy Reculver personality briefly struggled to the surface of her body and managed to say a few words before Georges Leon forced her back out of the driver's seat. I think it's something like vertigo, fear of falling—if you get pushed out of your own body, God knows how far you'd fall! And into what. And who would it be, exactly, that was falling? It's probably an unhealthy attitude, but I think I assume I'm defined by all my tastes and prejudices and weaknesses, and that if I were to lose them I'd dissipate like unconfined smoke. And it's a short step to attribute the same kind of defining-status to one's own physical body, with its quirks and tastes and limitations—take that away, and what's left? Well, we'll each find out eventually, but the idea is like walking on the railing of a very high balcony.

NG: You're a writer of novels delineating vast conspiracies behind historical and contemporary appearances; how deep does your personal paranoia run?

TP: Actually, it's all recreational! I turn it on when I'm composing stories, and when I'm reading Pynchon or the *Illuminatus* books, say, but in my day-to-day life I trust newspapers and history books. I mean, I like to balance a liberal newspaper with a conservative one, but between them I think I get a fairly accurate picture of the world. There are things I hope are true—I was all for cold fusion when it looked as if it had occurred, and I like to think there's an alien spacecraft at Area 51 in the desert—and I'm sure the Shroud of Turin is real—but if these are proven false, as apparently cold fusion has been, I don't cling to them and figure the Illuminati are hiding the real truth.

NG: Your first two novels, *Forsake the Sky* and *Epitaph in Rust*, were published in less than ideal circumstances. How did your experience there shape the remainder of your career?

TP: The Laser Books experience has just made me more tolerant of the behaviour of subsequent publishers. Laser was quick and high-handed—they'd re-write your stuff, and maybe or maybe not pay attention to corrections you made in the galleys. But they *did* publish me, when I was writing stuff that probably no one else would have published—and without that early reassurance I might not have gone on trying to write books. I do still like those two books, by the way! Probably more sentimentally than objectively, but I think they're not bad work for a 23-year-old!

NG: Your third novel, *The Drawing of the Dark*, was a huge leap forward in substance and technique. It was conceived as part of a multi-author King Arthur sequence, wasn't it? And from the Arthurian mythos, you seem to have derived an abiding interest in the figure of the Fisher King, reincarnating him in sundry of your novels . . .

TP: A British publisher was said to want a series of ten novels about King Arthur being reincarnated throughout history, and Jeter, Ray Nelson and I agreed to write them. After we had each written one or two, it turned out that the British publisher was *not* interested in any such series, and so the three of us were left to try to sell these odd books. I came across the Fisher King myths while researching Arthur—and yes, I have found them fascinating! It was fun to be able to return to the subject, solo and with no restrictions (and at more length!), in my [recent] trilogy.

The main reason *The Drawing of the Dark* was a better-put-together book than my previous ones had been was not simply because I had discovered the advantages of historical research—mainly it was because that book wound up in the hands of one of the truly great editors in our field, Lester del Rey. He made me re-write the daylights out of the original version I sent to him, and he taught me a whole lot about how a book works.

NG: Apart from your apprentice works, *Dinner at Deviant's Palace* is your only novel with a future—in this case post-apocalyptic—setting. Why did you choose to transplant ancient myth in this fashion?

TP: It was Orpheus and Eurydice, right! In fact, in an early draft it wasn't "Barrows" brandy, but "Dice," and so her name was Uri Dice, i.e. Eurydice, though pronounced differently. Later that seemed too cute. Anyway, I had always loved the post-apocalyptic setting, in books like George Stewart's *Earth Abides* and Edgar Pangborn's *Davy*, and so I wanted to play with all that myself. Having done it, though, I find I like the restrictions of actual history better—I need something pretty solid to push against.

NG: Speaking of which: *On Stranger Tides*, your novel about Edward Teach and fellow buccaneers, has a merry time with pirates and Vodoun. How much deliberate homage to past pirate literature is there in this novel?

TP: Well, there's homage to Rafael Sabatini, certainly, especially to his novels *The Black Swan* and *Captain Blood*. And to Robert Louis Stevenson. But I've tried not to make it overt, at all—I want it to be a synthesis of so many sources that you can't tell precisely what any of them were.

NG: More central to your historical direction: in parallel with Jeter and Blaylock, you cultivated throughout the Eighties the so-called Steampunk line of historical fantasies, neo-Victorian supernatural adventure tales of remarkable audacious artifice. Why this 19th Century orientation? To what do you attribute the especial excitement of historical fantasy generally?

TP: I guess Jeter started it, with his book *Morlock Night*; certainly he made up the term "steam-punk." But we had all been fans of Dickens and Stevenson and Arthur Conan Doyle, and 19th Century London is just a terribly attractive location for a story—echoes of Jack the Ripper, Jekyll and Hyde, Byron in Covent Garden, Boswell and Johnson wandering around bickering, and the whole mythology attached to the Thames! As for historical fantasy in general, I've found it to be a very fertile field. You get a colourful world ready-made, consistent in its technology, economics, architecture, politics, weaponry, and so forth—exotic because of being historical, but at the same time firmly moored in the real world (which fantasy desperately needs to be).

NG: When writing such historical fantasies, verisimilitude is important; yet you wisely avoid archaisms, especially in your dialogue. To what extent are your historical characters figures of their own time, and to what countervailing extent our contemporaries in period costume?

TP: Good question, because—especially if you take it back very far in time, as in *The Drawing of the Dark*—people of previous centuries really were very different from people today, in how they thought and how they regarded the world. They genuinely esteemed chastity in the Middle Ages, for example, and the default-opinions of our own moment in history make us read their attitude as hypocrisy or irony. So, frankly, it's a compromise—and somewhat involuntary. The characters are inevitably going to have some 20th Century perspectives that they wouldn't really have had, but I do try to immerse myself in the history & literature of a period enough to get at least some of their perspectives and ways of thinking. Interestingly, you find that each age has its own areas of clarity and its own blind-spots, including our own—you learn that some of the old philosophies were better in many ways, more accurate, than our own. I don't like reading historical fiction that too-clearly reveals its date of writing! Like, right now we see novels set in the past, or in imaginary lands, and the concerns are all very 1990s—women's rights, gay rights, child abuse, racial injustice, etc. Not that these things aren't important, but it's jarring to see them imposed whole, in recognizably contemporary terms, on another culture.

And sometimes I find that a long-ago culture is just too alien, in its thinking and attitudes, for me to put myself into its people. Once I was going to write a book about Francois Villon, but the casual, callous brutality of the time was just too off-putting; I'd have had to really force a whole lot of 20th Century (or at least 19th Century!) attitudes on the characters in order to write about them at all, and it would have been transparently inaccurate.

NG: Many people still regard *The Anubis Gates* as your finest novel; of the Steampunk books, I have a firm preference for *The Stress of Her Regard*. Which of your Eighties books satisfies you the most?

TP: That would be very difficult to say. I'm very fond of each of them! But I suppose *The Anubis Gates* is probably the best of them—I get a hint from the fact that it's been the most successful—and I can only guess at why. Maybe because Beth Meacham was my editor, and had a good eye for what bits needed cutting! But each of them has bits I'm very pleased with. Maybe *The Stress of Her Regard* is my favourite—I do like my vampires, and it was a lot of fun being able to have Byron on stage so much.

NG: Coming now to your Nineties work: your three novels of that decade are set in the contemporary USA. How difficult was the transition from fantastical historical reconstruction to this (still supernatural) modern verisimilitude?

TP: Really I'd always meant to write contemporary fantasy—the historical thing was a fortuitous discovery that I spent ten years exploring. It's fun—kind of a relaxation—to write about TVs and telephones and freeways, and to weave a supernatural story into them. I don't really find that I'm doing anything very different. Maybe because I got used to doing historical research, I find that I treat even present-day Los Angeles as a "historical" setting, which I've got to research the history and background of. I think I believed less research would be required for contemporary books, but that hasn't proved to be the case! One thing that I don't think I'll ever change is the supernatural element. I just don't seem able to think up any sort of plot that doesn't involve magical events somewhere.

NG: I for one was very surprised when *Last Call* and *Expiration Date* turned out to be the opening episodes of a trilogy, their casts of characters uniting in *Earthquake Weather*. Why did you structure these books this way? Do you think *Earthquake Weather* suffers from depending (uniquely among your novels) on acquaintance with previous books for its success?

TP: I knew that there were sequels attached to *Last Call*—a Fisher King has to die, after all, it's part of his story—but I wasn't sure I'd write them next. So I let *Expiration Date* appear to be an independent novel, in case I didn't get around to finishing the set for a while; and it was kind of fun to sneak the second book of a trilogy past everybody without making it appear to be that at all. *Earthquake Weather* was *meant* to be comfortably readable entirely on its own! My model was C. S. Lewis's *That Hideous Strength*, which works fine as the third of a trilogy or as a novel all by itself. Unfortunately, I gather that *Earthquake Weather* does *not* work that way. If I had it to do over again, I'd have one publisher for the three of them, and I'd have called them Volumes I, II, and III!

NG: I was often struck reading this contemporary/Fisher King trilogy—as I was in the case of Blaylock's quite similar *The Paper Grail*—by a sense that these books were commentaries on the Matter of America, the country's spiritual, political, and environmental nature and destiny. How correct is this perception?

TP: Well, I love the idea that they might work as that! But if they do, it's only accidental. I mean, if you're writing at length about contemporary America, I suppose a lot of your personal opinions and perspectives *will* filter through! I'll have to re-read the books and see what my opinions were! Being inadvertently-revealed like that, they're probably more sincerely-felt than what I consciously imagine my opinions are. It's no coincidence that Blaylock's *The Paper Grail* feels similar to my trilogy! We were both researching the Fisher King at that time, swapping reference books and reading each other's stuff, and so there was probably a lot of cross-pollination.

NG: Your short stories, gathered in *Night Moves*, read remarkably like your novels, only in miniature: they are as complex, only in especially distilled form. How demanding do you find short fiction writing, and why do you produce so little?

TP: I spend almost as much time outlining a short story as I do a novel—well, not really, but they're comparable. And then I find I want to compress too much into a short story, so that if I don't watch out it's going to be a sort of telescoped novel. Characters tend to arrive at decisions too quickly, from too little evidence. I was a bit nervous about trying to write a whole novel, the first time, but I found it was a relief to have all that room! And so I mainly think in novel terms these days, novel-size stories, and only do short-stories if somebody really pushes me to.

NG: Your most recent novel, *Declare*, is an astonishing book on any number of levels, an authentic masterpiece. How did you—how do you—strike upon these extraordinary, strange yet inevitable, connections? In *Declare*, the Cold War and the Arabian Nights, the SIS and Mount Ararat? You have a genius for these webs of subtle implication . . .

TP: That's very nice of you to say, and I owe you a drink! It starts with me being struck by something I read—not research reading, just recreational stuff, newspapers or biographies or histories—and it occurs to me that a book might be woven around whatever bit it is that's caught my attention. So I read another book or two about that. In the case of *Declare*, it was the odd life of Kim Philby—I wound up reading several books about him, without really deciding I would write about him myself. Then I started seriously looking for clues to the kind of story I write—that is, supernatural. And if you approach extensive research with this almost schizophrenic polarity, you do start to find that sort of evidence! I wind up convincing myself sometimes, if it's real late at night.

NG: Does *Declare*, even while it renders such splendid homage to John Le Carre, also subvert his mode of thriller writing? Turning as it does the history of espionage into a far deeper sort of secret history?

TP: Well, I suppose it does. The themes and points of Le Carre's fiction are widely at odds with my own, I think, even though we're using the same paint-box. His stories are resolutely about the world as it really is, and mine are just as resolutely about the world as it really is not. I just hope our audiences can overlap!

NG: With *Declare*, you stand at a rare pinnacle of novelistic achievement, a point of high thematic, stylistic, and technical maturity. Where do you go from here? More specifically, will your future characters down as much beer and ale as their predecessors?

TP: Speaking of which, I owe you another drink. Well, Blaylock and I have written a cookbook. Maybe we'll take on Hazan, Child and Beard! Actually, though, the next book is underway, and I hope it's good. I've got to admit I'm pleased with *Declare*, and the next one may or may not please me as much—right now it looks very good to me!—but if it doesn't, maybe the one after that will. I don't think I'll ever stop writing supernatural stories; somehow that's the only sort of plot I can think of. It comes from obsessively reading that stuff in my youth! And certainly my characters will continue to drink! I'm an Irish Catholic, so to me there's something powerfully spiritual about alcohol!

ELECKTRA DREAMS
Geoffrey Maloney

Towards the end of a long hard summer where the sea level rose to dangerous levels in the city, and hot winds blew deserts of red sand in from the west, my mother became ill and died quite suddenly. She had internalised the afflictions of the city as if they were an attack on herself, and I had felt powerless in the face of these things. I could shovel the sand out of her backyard, but I could do nothing about the cancer that had killed her, nor the rising waters that flooded the city.

On the morning of her funeral, I waited at the cemetery gates half-hoping, half expecting that my father would suddenly appear as if he had never been away. I imagined that he would slap me on the back, take me by the arm and lead me over to the freshly dug earth where the burial was to take place . . .

" . . . but your father," my mother said as she lay in her hospital bed with clear plastic tubes threading from her body to bags and machines of various kinds, "is a dry little creature, an ancient thing that has been kept hidden away, well out of reach of the world for many years."

I had wanted to say that perhaps my father was alive and well, or even that he was a tragic alcoholic living under a railway bridge somewhere, sitting there quietly in the dark, scribbling obscure poetry in a notebook that only he would ever read, but all I said was, "Don't upset yourself. He's not worth talking about."

But she paid no attention, perhaps she hadn't heard. "He is very short," she continued, "perhaps not even a foot tall, and his skin is very white, cracked and flaky, like the desiccated skin of an Egyptian mummy found in some tomb in the desert. He lives in a shoebox where once were kept . . . "

"Don't worry about him, stop thinking about him, he's not worth it, try to get some rest." False futile words not even worth uttering. But still I had said them.

I felt a presence behind me and turned to see one of the gravediggers in his dirty green dungarees beckoning me. "We can't wait any longer," he said. "We have other graves to dig." But he lowered his eyes when he said this, as if in show of respect. He meant no offence. He had work to do. I was one of many in the queue. There had been too many deaths that summer.

The red dust swirled around me, turning the sky to a fragile pink. The gravedigger led me through the lilac air to a deep and empty grave. It looked like a wound in the earth, a mouth that was ready to devour anything that was offered, the dust, the sea, the bodies that had failed. It was when the gravediggers were encouraging me to throw the first handful of dirt onto the coffin that I became aware of another person standing close by. I caught a glimpse of long blonde hair in the corner of my eye. But the gravediggers had shown such respect that I feared to turn my head until their business was over. I watched intently as they ploughed their shovels and piled the dry brown earth upon the coffin.

When they had finished, I turned away and saw a young woman walking quickly towards the cemetery gates. Her fine blonde hair streamed out behind her, catching the dust in the air.

"You knew my mother?" I asked when I caught up with her.

Her eyes were green, her nose was sharp, but her lips were dry and had begun to crack. Some blood seeped to the surface. My hand reached into my pocket and pulled out a tube of lip balm. I delicately traced the smooth gloss across the surface of her lips.

When I realised what I had done, I looked down at the tube of balm, then quickly returned it to my pocket. "A habit that my mother taught me," I said.

"Your mother was a friend of mine," she said, her hand rising to her mouth, her fingers delicately touching her lips.

"I didn't know she had any friends," I said. It was a simple truth.

"I used to visit her sometimes. We used to talk a lot."

"What did you talk about?"

"You mostly," she said, smiling in a fragile way. "She talked about you often."

I felt a flush rising to my cheeks.

"And sometimes your father," she said quickly as if to help me with my embarrassment.

I nodded my head. Always my mother would talk about my father. I had grown tired of her telling me how I would turn out just like him, if I wasn't careful.

•

Her name was Elecktra. Once it had been a fashionable name, a name bestowed upon sparkling young daughters by modern young parents. I gave her a lift home, to a house in Abbortsford not far from where my mother used to live. It was in a neighbourhood where the sea had already begun to lap at some doors, but people feared to move away because they still believed that their property was worth so much. The two of us held a wake for my mother, drinking wine from a cask and doing our best to speak about her virtues. She had been a meticulous woman, her house had always been neat, so clean, she had had a lot of sorrow in life. Some of which was true, some of which wasn't, but we embellished her virtues to the greatest degree possible as befitted the occasion. I did not pry into how well she knew my mother or why she had attended the burial. I was just happy to have somebody to share my mother's death with. If my father had been present, I would have imagined the two of us getting drunk in a pub somewhere—he telling me about all the things he'd done while he was away and I telling him about all the things that he had missed.

There came a moment, however, between Elecktra and I, when we had drunk perhaps too much wine and exhausted everything that we had to say. In that moment my eyes wandered and I noticed the red smudge Elecktra had left upon her glass when she took her lips away. Elecktra took a white handkerchief from her pocket and touched it gently to her mouth. That simple action brought a sense of déjà vu. Barely remembered images of the past drifted through my mind. There was a party when I had been younger. I had been carrying a tray of smoked oysters . . . Then the memory was gone and in its place I found my mother saying . . .

"Occasionally, she takes him out. She places his head in her mouth and slowly draws the life out of him . . . "

"For what purpose?" I had asked, wishing to humour her.

"To restore her beauty, of course, and her health." This said with such a knowing smile on her face as she lay dying.

"It's a condition I have," Elecktra said, not looking at me, but at her glass as she wiped the red smudge away with her handkerchief. "In places, the skin on my lips is very thin. At times the slightest pressure—when I drink, or perhaps a kiss—squeezes out a little blood. Not all the time, just sometimes are worse than others."

The déjà vu returned. "Look at her glass. See how she leaves lipstick traces there, look at the red smudge on the end of her cigarette. She's the slovenly type, dirty and cheap."

"My breasts too," Elecktra said. "My nipples. The skin tissue is the same . . . "

"Sorry?" I said, finding my memories vanishing. The smell of smoked oysters and hospital beds lingered in the air.

Elecktra laughed, blushed, then said, "I don't know why I'm telling you this. You find it disturbing."

"No, not at all," I said and thinking that she was about to cry I went to her. I knelt next to her, took her chin in my hand and kissed her gently on the cheek, then softly on the lips. With the tip of my finger I delicately traced the outline of her nipples beneath her soft cotton shirt. Then I unbuttoned her shirt, freed her breasts from the thin bra that she wore and kissed her gently on each nipple. I breathed in the sweet fragrance of her skin. Elecktra murmured something.

"Sorry," I said, moving quickly away, suddenly realising what I was doing, "sorry, I didn't mean, I . . . "

"It's okay," Elecktra said, quickly rearranging her clothes, "I could have said no . . . "

I smiled, nodded, muttered something about it being time to leave. At the door, she pulled me to her and kissed me warmly on the lips. "You didn't ask me," she said. "I thought you would, after what your mother said . . . it was the first thing I thought you'd ask."

"What?" I said, trying to imagine some innocent childhood intimacy my mother had revealed.

"Whether I know your father," Elecktra said. Now the tone of her voice had changed. She sounded disappointed, tense. It must have been something that my mother had said to her, some seed that she had planted. Perhaps because she had always feared that I loved my father more than I loved her.

"And do you know my father?" I asked.

"Yes," she said. "Last time I saw him he said that he wanted to see you."

"Whatever my mother told you was wrong," I said. "I loved her dearly. She never understood it but I did love her. My mother's problem was that she wanted my father to love her too. So whatever she told you, when she was sick, she seems to have confused me with my father. I don't care about my father; I never have."

Elecktra was still in the doorway staring at me as I drove away. She looked at me as though I had done something wrong and she had only been trying to help.

•

Elecktra and I lie in bed together. My hand reaches out to stroke her leg, but before I touch her skin, she arches her back and says, "Not tonight. I'm tired. I need to get some sleep."

"I wasn't thinking of sex," I whisper into the darkness, lying.

"Sssh," Elecktra says, "he might hear you. He's come home drunk again."

These words, so well understood, pass like a thought between us. A trapdoor opens and I fall through it. Elecktra is married to my father, and now on this bed she lies between us, fending off my father's drunken demands for sex and my more casual intimacies. After we became lovers, I thought she would stop sleeping with him, that they would no longer share the same bed. She had promised this. I feel sick inside and betrayed when I hear Elecktra say to him, "Okay, come on. Quickly. Get it over with."

I roll away from Elecktra's body, to the edge of the bed, lower myself to the floor, crawl across the carpet and creep out the door. I can hear my father's drunken grunts. I close my ears to Elecktra's sighs.

I woke with a cold chill in my body, filled with jealously, wondering why Elecktra had given in so easily. The wind roared outside, a vast huge cold wind that seemed to have blown up from Antarctica. It mingled with the red dust and seeped into the house through a crack in the bedroom window turning my toes to ice. As I tried to shake the dream from my mind, other memories intruded. There were people at a barbecue: my father, my mother, other men, women, pointed purple boots, a tray of smoked oysters . . .

It was a Saturday evening shortly before Christmas. My father in his role as the important supervisor had invited people from his office over for a barbecue and Christmas drinks. There were a few young women and men, some older men and their wives and several couples around my parents' age. There was one young woman in particular that I noticed and my mother noticed her too, even before she had time to finish her first drink. Perhaps it was the purple shoes that she wore.

"Look at her glass; she's the slovenly type," my mother said.

But this young woman did not strike me as a slovenly type. She had long dark hair and I thought that she was quite pretty. She laughed a lot, but there was something in her eyes that was dark and brooding, something that was mysterious and a little sad, as though she was waiting for something important to happen, but it never did. As the night progressed, I watched her more carefully and noted how she always checked her glass after she drank. She would look around to make sure that no one was watching, then use a white tissue to wipe away the red smear that had been left there.

"Watch your father," my mother said, "he can't resist these slovenly creatures."

It was true that my father was paying lots of attention to the pretty young woman with the serious eyes. He was in an exceptionally good mood, laughing and joking with her and she obviously enjoyed the attention. Some of the darkness left her eyes. They were no longer brooding; as if the thing she had been waiting for had finally happened.

"You're more like me, you look like me. Don't you ever turn out like him," my mother said and, in my innocence, I had assured her that I wouldn't.

But I could understand why my father found the young woman so interesting. I got close to her at one point and offered her a tray of smoked oysters and water crackers. While her fingers reached towards this offering, I was able to study her lips more closely. They were a deep natural red, almost raw it seemed to me and I was certain that she wore no lipstick . . .

My father left a few weeks later. We never saw him again.

I lay in bed listening to the howling wind. I had given her a smoked oyster to eat. Her skin was clear, her eyes were shiny, and her hair was full of lustrous dark curls. Elecktra's nipples had tasted salty and metallic in my mouth, slightly sweet, the taste of something wicked and illicit. I wondered why she had said the things that she had. She could not possibly know my father.

I left home early the next morning, just as dull night was giving way to dull morning. The streets were deserted and I felt that the whole city belonged to me. I planned to drive over to my mother's house, to put her things in order, but a short while later I found myself standing in Elecktra's backyard. I was gazing at a dying rose garden that was already partly submerged beneath the rising waters. There had been no answer at the front door. I wondered how much longer it would be before the water was inside the house.

I knocked on the backdoor and called out Elecktra's name. When no answer came, I put my ear to the door and listened. Inside it was still. I felt hot and foolish, told myself that I should leave, walk back to the street, climb in my car and drive away. Instead, I retreated slowly down the side passage trying each of the windows as I went. The third one I tried was unlocked.

•

It was an old fashioned bedroom, one that would have been more fashionable during the middle of last century than in these more modern times. A large double bed with a carved wooden headrest squatted against one wall. Opposite was a large oak wardrobe with oval mirrors in each of its doors, elsewhere a matching chest of drawers and a dressing table, a few simple pictures on the walls—flowers in Japanese vases, citrus fruits in ceramic bowls.

She knew my father. She did not know my father. I searched through her drawers looking for something that would reveal the truth. I found her underwear, the thin skinned bras that she wore,

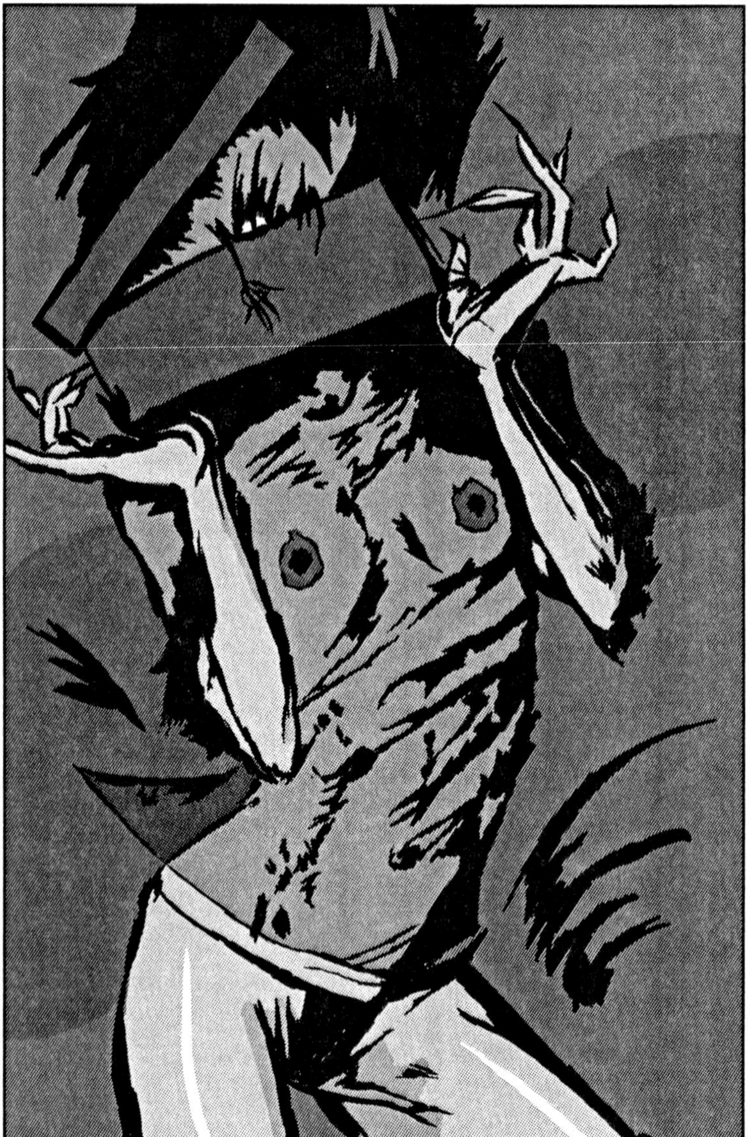

delicate lace panties, all containing a fragrance that reminded me of how her skin had smelt the night before. There was a finely crafted jewellery box containing several gold bracelets and rings with diamonds, emeralds and rubies; such expensive tastes for one so young.

I went to the wardrobe, rifled through her clothes—found one black dress after another, as if she felt comfortable in black and liked to wear it often. At the bottom of the wardrobe, I found a shoebox. I drew it to me and pulled the lid away. Inside there was a pair of purple suede boots. I crouched down and caressed them, feeling the soft suede beneath my fingertips.

"They're beautiful, aren't they?" The voice came from above. I turned my eyes to see a pair of slim white legs next to me, barely inches away from my cheek. I hadn't heard her enter. It was if she had been standing next to me all the time, just beyond my line of sight watching everything I had done. I swallowed back saliva. "You didn't answer the door," I said.

She crouched down next to me and kissed me on the cheek. Her lips were warm and soft. It seemed that we were friends again; perhaps we always had been.

"You'll need to move soon," I said. "The waters are still rising."

She touched the purple boots. "See how smooth they are," she said. "They don't make boots like this any more; these days the quality's just not the same."

"Where did you get them?" I asked.

She kissed me on the cheek again. Ran her fingers through my hair. "I promised your mother I would look after you, Stephen. She was worried that there would be nobody to look after you when she was gone."

The room grew suddenly claustrophobic. I felt that I couldn't breathe. I tried to stand up. Elecktra put a hand on my shoulder pushing me down. I was surprised by her strength.

"You missed something," she said. "Look here, look closer."

I looked back into the wardrobe and saw another shoebox hidden away down the back. It was similar to the one I already held, but it was a little more worn around the edges, as if it had been handled more often.

"Take it out," Elecktra said, "look inside."

She gave a wicked little laugh as I reached in for the other box. I held it in my hands. I could feel Elecktra's warm breath close to my face. The tip of her tongue traced a line across my cheek. "Where did you get the boots?" I asked again.

Her lips brushed my ear. She whispered, "Your father gave them to me."

I tried to laugh, but found that my throat had gone dry. I pulled the lid away from the shoebox quickly and looked down at the tiny creature that lay within.

I looked at Elecktra. A change had come over her. Her eyes were bright and shiny and her hair was full of dark lustrous curls. Her lips were blood red; they seemed almost raw. She wore no lipstick.

"Occasionally I take him out," she said.

"For what purpose . . . ?"

•

Elecktra is my wife. We make love in her bedroom, while the red dust swirls round her house and the waters rise in her kitchen. My father is neglected. He grows old in his shoebox. I open it from time to time. He still has all his hair, even though it is white and brittle. A silver crew-cut runs across the top of his head like the stiff bristles on a broom. He has shrivelled arms and shrivelled legs which are practically of no use at all. There is hardly anything left of him really; he's quite falling apart, all desiccated and dry, like a tiny little Egyptian mummy found in some far away desert. Just like my mother said.

TRAPDOOR
Darrell Pitt

The telephone rang.

"Son?"

My father's voice echoed distantly from the far side of the country.

"Yes. Dad. How are you?"

He cleared his throat. He always cleared his throat at the start of a conversation.

"Fine," he said. "And you?"

I told him I was keeping myself busy and had been leaving the house more often, the weather being the right side of perfect. The world was wonderful, and it was a joy to be alive.

"Yes," he said. "But how are you really?"

I took a deep breath, a deep shuddering inhalation that shook my ribcage and made my vision swim. Susan had been dead for three months, killed when a drunk driver slammed into our car, destroying the passenger side where she was sitting. I still felt lost, disassociated from the world, a ship without a port.

"Coping," I said to my father. "I'm doing better now, feeling better. Moving on."

"You can't blame yourself, son," he said.

"I know."

But I could blame myself, and I did. Susan had wanted to drive that night. If I had let her, she would have lived. I would have died, but that was a price I would have gladly paid. They say that life is in the details. So it was with Susan's death.

"I'm fine. Really."

And as I said the words I could hear the police radio, cracking like broken bones; I could see the light of the police car, soft and blue upon Susan's face, frozen in death, lost to life, lost to me.

My father and I spoke for another twenty minutes, but I don't remember a word we said.

•

I found the trapdoor later that day.

It was embedded in a recessed wooden frame in the roof of the upstairs hallway. It was made of five wooden slats; there was a knot in one of them. A roller brush had missed the bevelled edges of the timber, and pale pink undercoat peeked through like flesh.

I stood beneath the trapdoor and stared up. It had taken me by surprise. I had lived in this house for almost half a year, and I had not noticed it before. Up until now, I had lived like a ghost, existing but not living. I was a writer, and had published three novels before Susan's death, none of which were either good or bad. Now a single sheet had sat in my typewriter on the kitchen table for over a month. I had typed two lines.

Nothing is ever finished,

It just waits somewhere else.

I started up the ladder. It was a six-foot high metal ladder, the modern 'A' frame type. My head came level with the recess of the trapdoor. I pushed up. Nothing happened. I pushed again, and this time the trapdoor moved slightly. I took another step up the ladder, applied more force and the trapdoor swung upwards with a breathless groan. I let it fall back; particles of dust wafted down from the attic as it slapped back onto the wooden floor.

The room revealed itself to me slowly, like a woman undressing. The interior was dark, and an object was positioned next to the trapdoor. A trunk, a rusty red chest with a thin metal handle that would have a matching partner at the other end. I knew the type. I owned one just like it. A genuine boyish curiosity swept over me, momentarily flushing away the cobwebs of depression. There could be anything in that trunk, famous relics, lost jewels, hidden treasure. Maybe.

I gripped both sides of the hatchway, and pulled myself up into the room onto the cold dusty floor.

How interesting, I thought, as my eyes scanned the chamber. The attic looked very similar to the cellar downstairs. And it was full of belongings. Not empty at all. My heart began to thud. Hard. My throat constricted, and a high pitched wail echoed around in my head. I gripped the edges of the hatchway with shaking fingers, and looked down at my lap. After a moment I forced myself to look up again.

This room did not only look like the cellar of our house.

It *was* the cellar.

An unsteady smile played on my lips. Someone was playing games with my mind. They had reproduced our cellar in the attic, decorated the room with copies of our belongings. It was the only explanation.

But the explanation was ridiculous. I climbed to my feet. There was my old trunk, the red rusty one that I had owned since I was a boy, decorated with skull and crossbones, painted on it half a lifetime ago. Here: the hatstand in the corner; Susan had bought it impulsively from a market three years before. Over there, the storage cupboard that had only ever stored junk. Next to it was our old brown suitcase, tattooed with travel stickers from Rome and Paris, and sitting on top of *that* was a century-old copy of Romeo and Juliet, filled with pressed flowers from our wedding. And there, my toolbox, and next to that, our spare book shelf, filled with paperbacks, forever unread, but never orphaned.

It was a hoax. It had to be. I began to fume. Then I looked at the window at the far end of the room, and I knew that this was no hoax. The attic window was a single round pane of glass. This window was different, long, set high on the wall and divided into several panes. And here was the clincher.

There was grass growing outside it.

I staggered over to it. Impossible. I was looking across our garden. I peered past spindly rose bushes, watched a car crawl along the street, a woman jogger ran past our letterbox, her dog bouncing merrily behind her. Over the road, a man named Harris ran his mower across an uneven lawn.

This was no hoax.

I gave a sudden hysterical giggle that I slammed shut with my fist pressed into my mouth. I staggered back to the trapdoor, swung myself onto the ladder, almost tipped it over, stumbled down a few steps, dragged the trapdoor shut, almost upset the ladder again, and slid down the remaining rungs like a drunk man.

I collapsed the ladder. I lay it against the wall, and fearfully stared up at the ceiling, expecting something to come crashing after me. I floundered down the hallway, past empty bedrooms, down the stairs. I threw myself in a trembling heap onto the kitchen table. I slumped there in a daze until I realised I could hear a lawn mower. I sat up fearfully, and looked out the kitchen window.

Harris was almost finished. As he reached the far end of his block he brought the grass cutter to a halt, and wiped his brow. A strange, choking sob broke from me. I shoved a fist into my mouth to kill it, drawing blood.

I hardly noticed.

•

The next two days were the longest of my life.

For most of the first day I was convinced that I had lost my mind. I lay in bed and stared up at the ceiling, my soul a well of misery. Near the end of that day, I raised myself from the dead, fearfully skirted under the trapdoor and brought myself back to life with cold pizza from the fridge. I reached the conclusion that I was having some sort of breakdown; my wife was gone, I was living a solitary life in a foreign neighbourhood. Something had to give.

On the second day I decided that I felt too well to be losing my mind. I sat in a coffee shop at the local mall, surrounded by the circus of everyday life, and drank black coffee loaded with sugar. Boys and girls with pimples scanned grocery items at a nearby supermarket, and occasionally I heard a tinny booming voice, directing other pre-pubescent children towards aisles choked with human traffic. Women trundled by with shopping trolleys, children in their wake. Old couples wandered past, hand in hand, lost in the autumn of their lives.

I wasn't insane. Then what? It was not a hoax; it could not be an optical illusion. My eyes settled on a picture in a framing shop on the other side of the mall. It was a M.C. Escher drawing. A man walks up a set of stairs, turns and ascends another, and then another, and finally arrives back at the place where he started. The imagery brought me some peace.

Space folded inside my house, just as it did in that picture.

I was not insane.

I wasn't.

•

I awoke early the next day, a new man, determined to face whatever lay beyond the trapdoor. I tried to write a note in case the attic/cellar swallowed me whole, but words failed me. I couldn't decide what to write without sounding like a madman. I abandoned the pen and blank page on the kitchen table.

I walked outside and did a loop of the house. This was suburbia, the patchwork land of lawn and detached housing. Two children rode by on bicycles. The woman next door, with an unpronounceable Romanian name, was planting a bed of marigolds in her front yard. She gave me a wave.

I crossed to the middle of the front yard, and looked up at the attic window. The interior of the room was in darkness. I padded over long grass and fell to my knees at the cellar window. The room looked completely ordinary, except for the trapdoor next to my old trunk. I was sure it had not been there before. Re-entering the house, I walked upstairs, put up the ladder and climbed up again.

I pushed up the trapdoor. As it swung open, I told myself that my next sight would be an attic, a room that I had never seen before. It had to be.

Of course, it wasn't.

Already I could see the flat cellar roof, supported by bare wooden beams. I raised my head into the enclosure. There it was; trunk, hat rack, cupboard, suitcase, window, all enshrouded in dust. I stood up in the silent room, having just accomplished the impossible, covering the distance from cellar to attic in a split second. I walked the length of the room, touching a few objects at random.

There was only one place to go from here. I walked up the cellar stairs, and pulled open the door that led to the downstairs hall. I wandered up and down the hall twice, checked the lounge room, inspected the kitchen, walked out onto the front lawn, and gave the Romanian woman another wave. I circled the house again. I went inside to the kitchen.

I made a sandwich and started to eat it. A strange exhilaration swept through me, a new confidence.

I was not insane.

I abandoned the half eaten sandwich, and kept on going, transporting myself from one end of my house to the other a further eight times.

After that the novelty wore off.

I felt great; better than I had felt in a long time. I sat down in the kitchen again, and tried to collect my thoughts. It might help if I made notes. I stiffened. Where were the pen and paper that I had placed here earlier? My eyes swept the table. And where was my sandwich? I had left the half-eaten remains here barely an hour earlier. A cold dread gripped me as my eyes settled on the typewriter. Below the two lines of text, a new line had been added.

It goes on forever,

My head swam with fear. There was an intruder in my house. Arming myself with a knife, I searched the building, ready to defend myself against whoever had invaded my sanctum. I checked window and doors, searched under beds and inside cupboards, found nothing. I made my way to the attic.

I ascended the ladder, knife in hand and climbed up into the cellar. I sat down on the trunk, my new self-assuredness quickly wavering. Maybe I was crazy. Do the insane know they are insane?

A sound came from below. And another. Footsteps. Someone was coming up the hall. I backed away from the hatch, the hairs stiffening on the back of my neck. The ladder shuffled and creaked. My breath stopped. My heart was in my throat. I held the knife tighter, ready to attack. The top of a head appeared. Their face followed. They looked up.

Time stopped. There was no movement. No sound. If a bomb had exploded at that instant, I would not have noticed. I opened my mouth to speak, but no words came. He climbed into the cellar.

He was me; he was a duplicate copy, a doppelganger; he had my eyes, my hair, my height and build. His face was filled with astonishment.

"Who—" I started.

"What—" he said.

We stopped.

"You first," I volunteered.

He let out an exasperated sigh and spread his arms.

"What the hell's going on?" he asked

Listening to a recording of yourself is usually disconcerting enough. Hearing my voice come out of someone else's mouth was ultimately stranger.

"Let's go upstairs," I suggested.

We went to the kitchen.

We were not alone. Another copy of me was sitting at the kitchen table. He stared at both of us with such an expression of amazement that it was almost amusing. He had made sandwiches, and his mouth hung open, filled with the half-eaten contents.

The version of me that I had met in the cellar was the first to speak.

"We don't know what's going on either," he said.

Silence dragged on.

"Coffee?" I suggested.

As I dragged out cups, I began to number my counterparts. The one I had discovered in the cellar was number two. The kitchen version of me was number three. Number two boiled water as I heaped coffee into cups. By the time we sat down at the table together, I had formulated an explanation.

"Parallel universes," I offered. The others nodded in agreement. The same thought had obviously been dawning on them too.

"It's like a mass of spider webs," number two said. "Every action produces a multitude of other realities. I haven't just been transporting from one end of the house to the other. I've been shifting realities."

Number three continued. "The further we get from our own realities, the more different they become."

"The pen, paper and half eaten sandwich—" I started.

"I wondered where they came from," number two said.

"And now we've caught up—" number three began.

"A backlog—" I said.

Movement in the doorway. Another version of me—of us—stood there, staring at us with amazement.

"Parallel universes," number two said by way of rapid explanation. "Let's move to the lounge room."

More of me—more of us—turned up over the next hour. Some appeared in groups of two and three. One enormous group of six appeared together, looking for all the world like old friends. Eventually there were twenty-four of me in the room. Some were bearded. Some had different haircuts. Some were more like me, some less. They settled into three large groups while a few pottered individually around the room, picking out little differences between this reality and their own. I lifted up a framed photo. In this reality it was a photo of Susan. In my house—my reality—the photo was of both of us.

An idea occurred to me, a wild, fantastic idea. My head spun. I felt numb at the possibility. I casually made my way to the exit and passed two more versions of myself entering the room.

As I went up the stairs to the first floor, I heard a scuffle.

"Don't try to stop me," I heard a version of myself say.

Another version of me gave an anguished cry.

I rounded the stairs, looked down the hall and saw two of me grappling on the floor. One of them had a gun. It spat and a bullet whined past my face. My unarmed duplicate looked up at me with desperate eyes. I ran forward and struggled the gun out of his counterpart's grip.

I raced to the ladder, the strange weapon in my hand. I knew what the wild, incredible idea was that had occurred to my counterparts. It was the same idea that had occurred to me, and would eventually occur to all of them. There was the rumble of feet on the stairs. I ascended the ladder and climbed into the attic that wasn't an attic, and dragged the ladder up after me while waving the gun wildly at the crowd below.

I looked down at their stunned faces.

"Don't follow me," I said in a surprisingly clear voice. "I'll use violence, deadly violence on anyone who follows. I mean it."

I closed the trapdoor with a bang, and heard chaos erupt from below. I dragged the cupboard over the trapdoor, knowing it was a futile act. They would find a way through. They would never give up. I knew I wouldn't.

There had to be a reality, somewhere, out of all the multitudes of realities, where I drove the car that night and Susan didn't, where she lived and I died. Somewhere out there she was grieving for me, wanting me, needing me.

I started towards the stairs.

THE FACELESS MAN
Gene O'Neill

I first glimpsed the faceless man the night the *Elephant Seals*' trainer, Benton LaChapelle, called me about our basketball team's power forward, Damon Brown.

LaChapelle had called late in the afternoon, about five or so, just as I was about recovered from the after-game excitement of last night's win in Aptos against Cabrillo Junior College, our arch-rival.

"Hello, Stan? This is Benton. I just left Dr Hennessy's."

"Yes," I said warily, for I could read the bad news in his tone. And of course I knew Hennessy was the leading orthopaedic surgeon in the County, perhaps even in all of Silicon Valley just over the Santa Cruz Mountains.

"It's worse than we thought," he said with a heavy sigh.

"How bad, Benton?" I asked, hoping it would only mean the boy was out for two or three weeks. If that were the case we might hang onto first place for a short time; we were moving into the soft part of our league schedule—

"Doctor Hennessy says the MRI shows only a minor cartilage tear but extensive ligament damage to the knee. Damon will need major surgery, so we can forget just 'scoping."

"Oh, man, there goes my whole season, right down the frigging tubes," I said, not even trying to stifle the self-serving sense of self-pity in the statement. After ten years of coaching high school over in the Valley, I'd finally landed the basketball coaching job at Año Nuevo

College, a new school that competed in the Central Coast League, the toughest junior college circuit in Northern California. I was on my way up. And after recruiting Damon Brown, a blue-chipper from Dorsey High in L.A., I knew our team, the *Elephant Seals*, had a chance for a championship my first year, maybe even a shot at the State Junior College title. And then? Well, who knew what might happen?

But now—

"Yeah that's really tough luck for you, Stan," LaChapelle said, not even trying to hide the heavy sarcasm. "Damon will probably never play basketball again. In fact the doctor isn't too sure the boy will ever be able to walk comfortably again."

"Hey, don't get me wrong, man, that is too bad about Damon," I said, trying to backfill a little. "Damn, if *we'd* only known . . . " I had intentionally stressed the we. LaChapelle, as the team trainer and a registered physical therapist, had initially resisted my wanting to play Damon against Cabrillo College, after the boy had sustained a knee injury in practice during the week. But even though his mobility was effected by the injury, Damon was competitive, tough, and wanted to play in the critical game. So LaChapelle finally relented, concurring with my judgement that it was a minor hyperextension and strain. He taped the boy and supplied the light brace for the big game against Cabrillo. We'd won, but Damon was limping badly in the second half, and we had to take him out. By the end of the game he couldn't walk. So, LaChapelle had taken him to the hospital for X-rays, then contacted Dr Hennessy, who set up an appointment the next day to have the knee imaged.

We talked a few more minutes, LaChapelle ranting and raving about our responsibility for aggravating the injury; and if we had only taken the boy in for imaging after it first happened in practice and on and on. I maintained all along that we were dealing with two *separate* injuries, one minor in practice, the major one happening in the game. But LaChapelle wasn't buying that line. Didn't matter. I figured so frigging what. He had to deal with his own guilt, but he also had to go along with the programme, now, if he didn't want to destroy his career. So after listening to a few more minutes I finally begged off and hung up, looking out the window into the rain that was really coming down.

That's when I spotted him, the faceless man.

He seemed to appear suddenly like an apparition just beyond the pale illumination cast by the street lamp across the street from our house, the details of his body and face obscured by the shadows and heavy rain—or so I thought at the time. And from the position of his body I assumed that he was staring back up at my second-story office window. Just standing there in the rain near the streetlight, watching me. It was kind of a spooky, weird moment.

Who in the hell was this guy? I asked myself, still staring down through the heavy rain. We didn't have prowlers here in this community. Or even burglars. I looked around for a car, but there were none nearby, then I looked back to the streetlight.

He was gone!

In fact I wasn't sure I'd really seen him. After all, who would be out on a night like this, standing in the dark, staring up at me on the phone in my office? I shook my head. Forget it, man, it's just stress, I told myself. You've been wound a little too tight lately.

I tried to push the phone call and strange visit to the back of my mind, but I was pretty unnerved by it all . . .

The boy was almost shaking with dread as he waited for his foster father, the preacher.

Earlier in the afternoon, he had two young friends over to play in the back yard. But after a while they grew bored and decided to cross into the fenced-off garden area and play hide and tag. With a certain devilish delight they tunnelled through the huge tomato vines, so green and already heavy with young fruit. Oh, what fun it had been in there in the fuzzy, sticky, hot, green tunnels, hiding and seeking with his two friends. When they finally tired of playing the game, the three boys stood, staring and pointing at each other, laughing until tears rolled down their cheeks, for each of them wore telltale green stains on their arms, faces, and clothes from their romp among the sticky vines. When they stopped laughing the three boys stared out into the garden at the vines that were now broken, crushed, and flattened, many of the young tomatoes knocked off the plants; and their mood quickly sobered. After his friends' speedy departure, the boy, now left alone with the devastation, sucked in a deep breath and shuddered, an icy hand gripping his heart, for he suddenly remembered that the tomato plants in this garden plot always produced prize-winning tomatoes for the county fair each year.

So he was indeed frightened, waiting for the preacher to finish at the New Dawn Church of the Living Gospel next door, come home, and discover the destruction . . .

A few minutes later, feeling a little better, I went into the family room, where Lily, my wife, and Kim, our ten-year-old daughter were watching a movie on TV.

Lil must've read my expression—she had her questioning look.

"Damon's out for the season," I explained, then added, "and he'll need reconstructive surgery. May not play any more."

"Oh, no," she said, shaking her head sympathetically. "His mother must just be worried sick."

I nodded, then said, "Maybe I'll go over and visit them." Mrs Brown, a widow, had moved from L.A. to Santa Cruz when Damon decided to attend our school. And I'd managed to get him a job on the Boardwalk, an amusement park in Santa Cruz, and his mother a position in the housekeeping department of Sea Breeze, a local nursing home. They were doing okay, but their long-range financial future was dim if Damon's basketball career was over.

"Do you want me to come along?" Lil asked. She didn't know anything about the history of Damon's injury.

"No, Babe, I'll do it."

I returned to the office and made a call to Mrs Brown.

•

From that point on, the season went into a downward spiral. We lost most of our remaining games, even the easy ones. It wasn't just Damon, either. The team probably sensed the tension between Benton LaChapelle and myself, and some of them might've even guessed the general nature of the problem. The San Jose' Mercury picked up on the dissension, the sportswriters second-guessing every decision—starting lineups, substitutions, game strategy, everything I did. The *Elephant Seals*, unlike their namesake, made no comeback; we went down the tubes. And paralleling the decline was a kind of deterioration of my home life. Things got pretty strained with Lil.

And that's when I began to have lunches and take walks at the J. C. with Allie Gerosa, the ladies' volleyball coach. She seemed to be so understanding. Of course, at the beginning, I convinced myself it was all very innocent, nothing personal really.

At the end of Allie's season, which overlapped mine because she'd made the State playoffs, we were both scheduled for a presentation to the College Board, summing up the first seasons for both teams, going over future budgets, etc. Allie, who commuted over the mountains from San José, ate with us at home, meeting Lil for the first time. She was bubbly and excited about her new job—at the end of the semester she was taking over the woman's volleyball program at San José State.

We left about 7:00 p.m. for the meeting. Then, after surviving the presentation we decided to have a celebration drink, Allie and I.

That night was the real beginning of the whole mess, the big trouble.

Earl's Blue Note was a little bar not too far from the J.C. in a shopping centre that served the rural community north of Santa Cruz. It was kind of a funky Chicago-kind of nightclub, all black and white and chrome. In fact as Allie and I walked into the joint the jukebox was blaring, "Ain't No Sunshine When She's Gone," one of my favourite pieces by Bill Withers. We sat down at a table, Allie scooting into the booth close to me, our backs against the wall facing the bar, the jukebox to our far right. The place was nearly empty, one couple at the bar and a pair of single men peering dumbly at a boxing match on the TV near their end of the bar, the music not seeming to bother either of them.

We ordered a pair of margaritas and I made a toast when the drinks came. "To you, Ms Gerosa. All the best of luck at State," I said, touching her glass. "I know you'll do well there, too."

She leaned in close, her breast just touching my shoulder. "Thanks, Stan." She took a sip of her drink, still leaning against my shoulder. "Actually what I'm going to really miss is our lunchtime walks, you know what I mean."

I nodded, unable to ignore the electric eroticism of her contact. Actually she wasn't full-breasted—kind of flat—but she was wearing no bra, and I could feel the nipple of her breast burning into my arm.

Allie was a tall woman, almost six foot, her curves gently contoured to the athletic build of a dancer. Dark hair, dark eyes, and a big wide smile that exposed the whitest teeth. She was an attractive woman, no question about that, especially in her gym shorts—long, beautiful legs. The male P.E. staff called her *super-wheels*.

Finally, she eased away slightly, letting me catch my breath. We sipped the margaritas in silence, listening to the music, watching the other couple dance over near the jukebox. After some of the pointed questions from the Board during my presentation, it was a welcome relief. We chatted on about a number of things, mostly her situation. She was recently divorced and apparently recovering nicely, excited about fixing up an old farmhouse in San Jose´ she'd inherited from her grandparents. That was the reason she commuted—she loved the old place, which had been her home most of her life. And, of course, she talked about State—her goals, her ambition.

I didn't say much at that point, nothing about the basketball season, because there wasn't much to say. It had been a fiasco; and I'd be lucky to have a job next year.

After another round Allie talked me into dancing. She was as graceful as her appearance, and up close I could tell she wore no special scent. She needed nothing, her hair smelling fresh and clean, like the air after the first Fall rain. Of course I realised that something more was happening here than the casual flirting we'd engaged in at the end of the season. But I wasn't about to leave.

I asked her about male friends. She had none, at least no one special, which was hard to believe, but I didn't press.

Later, I glanced up and there was no one at the bar. I looked at my watch:12:45. Holy shit! I had a 7:45 a.m. fitness class in the morning. We must've been in the little bar for over three hours. Where had the time gone?

I stood up, tossed a few bills on the table for the waitress and took Allie's hand, saying, "It's after midnight. Would you believe it? I guess time does fly when you're having a good time; and I've had a great time, tonight, but I have to go home now." I shrugged.

She stood slowly and I could detect a funny look in her eyes—a sense of disappointment?

We walked back out to her VW bus and stopped. "I'll miss you, Stan," she said, then kissed me—a quick, wet, sexy kiss. When I opened the door for her, the light went on, and I saw the travelling case in the back seat and her freshly-pressed gym clothes on a hanger.

I said goodbye and was headed for my car before the significance registered . . . Then I stopped, turned around, and went back to the bus.

She rolled down the window and nodded, as if privy to my

thoughts.

"I'll call you, soon," I said hoarsely, leaned in, and kissed her again.

She understood.

I turned away and headed for my car, but before reaching the car door I stopped and watched the VW bus leave the parking lot. Only then did I really notice the weather—the fog had rolled in from the ocean and was so thick that I could only follow Allie's headlights down the road twenty yards or so. Then, quickly, I slipped into my car, started it, and turned on the defroster, glancing in the rear-view mirror—

That was when I saw him again.

The faceless man was standing at the corner of the building, near the neon sign: Earl's Blue Note, just barely noticeable in the thick mist. I knew he was watching me, but still I couldn't make out any details of his face or even what he was wearing.

He was just a shape in the fog.

I turned on my headlights, cranked the wheel hard right, made a 180 degree turn, aimed in his direction, gunned the accelerator . . . and for just a fleeting moment, I caught him in the glare of my lights—

Then he was gone!

Even though it had been too quick to digest details I had the distinct impression that his face lacked any features. That it wasn't just masked by the fog. But I was tired and had been drinking—in fact I felt oddly strung out. I shrugged the sighting off.

•

At first his foster father didn't say anything, his face an expressionless blank as always, only his eyes hinting at the inner fire raging in his soul, his penetrating gaze turning a chilling neon-blue as he stared down at the boy for a full minute. Then he shook his head, and he asked with just a hint of exasperation in his soft tone, "You knew better?"

The boy looked down at his feet and nodded.

"I asked, if you knew better?" the preacher said in his Sunday sermon voice.

The boy cleared his throat and looked up, the icy hand clutching his heart so tightly he could barely breathe. "Yes," he whispered, "it was wrong."

"And you realise you must be punished?" the preacher said, still looking down at the boy with his scary eyes.

"Y-Y-Yes," the boy stammered, fighting back the tears.

•

A few days later I visited Allie at her home in San José.

It was a great place, a white farmhouse perched on a little knoll, an anomaly surrounded by a brand new development that had displaced her grandparents' orchards. And Allie belonged in the house, moving about with a quiet, familiar confidence.

She had cooked us an Italian dinner, everything made from scratch; the old-fashioned kitchen where we ate pungent with the smell of tomato sauce, garlic, spices, and herbs, the memories of many, many other meals scratched in the cupboards, worn on the stovetop, and hacked into the old chopping block. We ate by candle-light on a red and white chequered table cloth, lingering over the Chianti, Allie's dark eyes glistening like ebony in the flickering light. It was a lovely meal . . .

A little later, in the bedroom, the slow grace of the evening was quickly abandoned as we undressed each other with a kind of frantic haste: dropping trousers, discarding a t-shirt, flinging a blouse, satiny-black bra abandoned. Her black panties clung to one ankle, everything else randomly littering the floor—

"Wait," I whispered hoarsely, pushing her away and peering at her nakedness.

She was indeed flat-chested, but her erect nipples were highlighted with very large, dark aureoles, and her skin so tan and smooth. I dropped my gaze, her long dancer's legs joining at a dark, thick, pubic bush.

For a moment I was frozen in place, stunned by her elegance in the dim light.

Then we were together and dropping to the floor.

With little foreplay I mounted her among the disarray of our clothes—two panting, sweating animals briefly locked together, guided by raw instinct . . . Much later, we made love in Allie's bed—slow, caring, thoughtful. Afterwards I got up and looked out her window at the moon, which was almost full—

And I saw him again, the faceless man.

He was down at the corner, near the closest split level, beneath the shadowy overhang of the building, gazing back up the hill at me. I drew back a step from the window, out of the moonlight. But he didn't react at all. Probably most people wouldn't have even noticed his presence there.

But I did; and I gasped aloud.

"What is it, Stan?" Allie asked, getting up with the sheet still wrapped around her.

"Nothing," I lied, glancing at her, then turning back to the window. "Just the moonlight. It's so beautiful."

He was gone!

"Oh, it is lovely," she said, putting her arm around my waist and hugging me close. "But you're cold. Look at the goosebumps along your arms."

I looked down at my arms and nodded, the past euphoria destroyed by the glimpse of the mysterious visitor. Who was he? Why was he watching me? I shuddered with a sudden rush of paranoia—

"You better come back to bed," Allie said, mistaking the shiver. "I'll warm you up." She smiled lasciviously.

I let her lead me back to the warmth of the bed, still obsessed with dread. Maybe I was under surveillance by a crafty investigator, I thought . . . But who would hire him? The insurance company for Mrs Brown. No, they wouldn't care what I was doing now. The J.C.? Maybe they were going to fire me, but they wouldn't need this. No, I finally decided, it must be Lily. It had to be my wife. She'd hired this guy to spy on me.

Much later, on the way back over the mountains to Santa Cruz, I decided to watch Lil. I knew that sooner or later she'd give herself away.

•

By the end of the month I was convinced I was correct; my wife had me under surveillance. I would come into a room and she'd hang up the phone abruptly, making obvious excuses for the behaviour; and her chequebook had check numbers unaccounted for. Nevertheless, I decided it was worth the risk to attend a three day P.E. conference at Sacramento State with Allie. She was conducting one of the workshops in volleyball. Of course we couldn't stay at the same hotel with most of the other P.E. people, too chancy.

But I solved the problem with the help of an old friend. I had played basketball at Sac State with Seamus Cavanaugh, before he flunked out and became a bartender. Now, he owned The Tradewinds Bar out in Orangevale, just north of Sacramento, and maintained an apartment over the place. It was the perfect spot to take Allie. We would see no one there we knew from the conference.

•

"Here's the key," Seamus said, winking at Allie who actually blushed. He was still the big overbearing handsome Irishman, maybe ten or so pounds heavier, but the same head of orange hair, engaging smile, and same blarney. "You'll need to dig up some fresh linen and towels out of the closet near the bathroom. Everything else should be okay. Eat and drink whatever's in the fridge. Come on down when you're ready for a real drink. I'll be on 'til two tonight . . . Hey, we got live music tomorrow." He proceeded to tell Allie a pair of jokes that added more colour to her cheeks; but I could tell she liked him. We stayed in the bar for quite awhile, before we went upstairs.

Later, we were lying in bed, listening to the traffic on distant Highway 50, the bar noises downstairs surprisingly quiet. That was when I had that funny feeling that raised the hair on the back of my neck, you know that creepy sense of being watched by someone out of sight.

I sat up suddenly, frightening Allie.

"What is it?" she asked, sitting up wide-eyed, with the sheet pulled up around her throat, hiding her nakedness.

"He's here." I whispered, putting my finger to my lips.

Then I eased out of bed, crossed the room, and pulled the drape open just a crack. I peered out into the night, checking the street below the window. There were a few cars out front, probably patrons of The Tradewinds, but no one on the street—

Something caught my eye.

He was standing back in an alley directly across the street. And It's likely I would've missed him if he hadn't shifted his weight slightly. But he was there, almost perfectly blended into the shadows. Then he moved a step forward into the light for a fleeting moment, and I got a good look at his face.

Nothing, only a pair of penetrating eyes!

"Get your glove."

"Glove?" the boy repeated, not understanding.

"The new one," the preacher explained and sighed, the resignation heavy in his tone. "The baseball glove."

Then the boy understood, and his legs went rubbery and unresponsive with dread as he shuffled into his bedroom for the treasured item—the new baseball glove with the Willie Mays signature. He was barely able to find it in his equipment box, his vision badly blurred by the tears he could no longer restrain.

When the boy returned, the preacher took the glove and explained in his holiest voice, "You must lose something that means a great deal to you." Then he waited a moment, until the fire he'd lit in the fireplace was roaring, and he threw the baseball glove into the flames.

"What is it, Stan?" whispered Allie, joining me at the parted drape, trying to see.

"It's him . . . in the alley across the street."

She peered into the night for a moment, then glanced at me with a puzzled expression. "I don't see anyone," she said, then looked again. "Who do you think is out there?"

"I know he's out there—"

He moved again!

"There," I said, nodding toward the alley, "did you see him move?"

"No," she replied, still looking, but frowning now. "Who is it?" she whispered, her tone demanding an answer.

"It's the faceless man," I said, feeling very rattled, tired, and disoriented.

"The faceless man?" Allie repeated, and she had that look people get—a cross between puzzlement and suspicion that they're really being put on.

I let the drape slide together. "Yes, he's been following me . . . us for some time."

"Who is he?"

I shrugged. "I'm not sure," I said. "Maybe a private detective. Who knows? Usually he never exposes himself, never leaves the shadows.

Thinks he's really fucking clever. But I saw him for sure tonight. Ha! No nose, no mouth, nothing!"

Allie frowned. "You mean you actually believe he has no face?"

I nodded.

She looked at me as if I'd just admitted to testing HIV positive.

"I'm pretty sure he has no features except for his weird eyes, a penetrating icy-blue gaze, you know." I described the night I caught him in the glare of the headlights. Then I began at the beginning, the first time I noticed him.

Allie listened patiently and her expression gradually turned to . . . a concerned pity. She tossed on her clothes. Finally she said in a gentle whisper, "Stan, you need some help. I'm going down to get Seamus."

She moved toward the door.

"No!" I said, grabbing at her shoulder. "The faceless man'll see you leave."

She slipped out of my grasp, and turned around to face me, speaking in her normal voice . "Yes, I'm going right now. You're confused, Stan, and you really need help." She went to the window and threw the drape open wide. "There's no one down there spying on us. See? No faceless man—he doesn't exist. I'm going to ask Seamus to come up and talk to you."

She had her back to me as she moved to the door and grabbed the knob.

"No," I cried, reaching out and clutching a fistful of her long hair. I jerked her backwards, the door slipping from her grasp and flying open. I slammed it shut and slid sideways, peeking out the window. "We can't let him know we realise he's watching," I whispered, glancing back at Allie after I eased the drapes shut. She was lying quietly on the floor.

"I'm going to go out and catch him, bring him back here. Make him talk to you. Then you'll know. You'll see. Wait here . . . "

It's difficult to remember exactly what happened after that. Kind of a blur.

I guess I was indeed kind of confused, left the apartment door wide open, then wandered around on the street, a great deal of time passing, most of the night or so. When I got back to the bar, it was dawn and they were all there—Seamus, paramedics, the police, reporters.

Allie was dead! She'd been stuffed under the bed.

I tried to tell them it must've been the faceless man that broke her neck, tried to hide her. But no one wanted to listen to that.

It was all one big mess.

The two, stood there and watched the wonderful glove slowly burn . . . turning black then dark grey and finally white as it transformed from something highly-valued to a worthless pile of ashes—the boy with the hot tears running down his cheeks, dripping off his chin, and the preacher with the penetrating blue gaze.

•

So, I live here now at Napa State Hospital, a really special kind of place. It's not too bad when you get used to it. I have my own Walkman, I listen to the games, the Warriors. Oh sure, I miss not being able to take long jogs, but I'm resigned to that now. They do let me shoot baskets every day on an outside court surrounded by a chain-length fence topped with razor wire. And the doctors are all pretty helpful, except they don't believe in the faceless man. They think I made him up—he exists only in my head.

They're wrong, I could never make up someone like him. He's with me all the time. Right now he's there in the corner, the shadows wrapped around him like a cloak, so no one can see if they glance through the observation port in the door. The faceless man never says anything; he just watches.

But of course I recognise him, those non-feeling, condemning eyes—like a pair of neon-blue stars sparkling coldly in the night sky.

WITHIN TWILIGHT
Chris McMahon

The Teacher was here.

Peter Jones 39 gave his homemade fire engine one last hug and stuffed it under a loose floorboard. If they discovered the toy he would be taken away for conditioning. He was in enough trouble as it was. Three days ago he had broken the Primary Rule. He had refused the data-dump from his father.

Maybe I can slip out, before they see me, thought 39. Carefully he tried to open the door. He was locked in! He rattled the door with all the strength of his eight-year-old frame. It would not budge. He knew that his grandfather, Peter Jones 37, had been strong enough to take the door off its hinges, but that did not help him now.

"I must consider an adequate response," he said to himself, scanning the wide landscape of data-dumped memories for some clue. The most recent were those of the board meeting—his father's memories—productivity quotas, staff problems. Beneath these were the hazy memories of Peter Jones 37, disjointed and fragmented. It was rare that secondary memories—a generation removed—survived intact, and there were only a score of memories from his grandfather that made any sense at all.

He jumped onto his bed, standing on tiptoe to stare into the garden. He had tried talking to old Jones through his data-eye, but he was hiding in the tree with his chariot.

The tree stood like a green flame sculptured from living tissue.

Peter Jones 38 had worked each one of those precise curves with an electric hedge trimmer, as had Peter Jones 37, and Peter Jones 36 before him—all the way back to Peter Jones 1. 39 knew each one of those tedious cuts—his father's memories were etched into his brain by previous data-dumps. Yet when the wind blew, and the sky darkened in twilight, the tree would come to life—surging and twisting into shape after shape until, finally, old Jones emerged, standing proud in his chariot. And the strangest thing of all: he could talk to old Jones.

Beyond the tree line, the sky was darkening.

"Please, let there be another storm. *Please*."

39 had noted a deterioration in his speech since he had refused the data-dump—and other strange feelings. He would sometimes giggle without warning—and at the strangest things.

He sighed and tried to see his parents' lounge room through the keyhole.

"It's getting worse," came the familiar voice of 38 through the door, "We have caught him with the junior-adults twice now, sharing eyes."

Then the voice of the Teacher, "Unauthorised data-dumps? Why weren't we notified?"

"Well, we were concerned, of course." 39 could hear the gruffness in his father's voice, hiding fear.

"The Department of Education has rules. They will be enforced."

Silence. Then his mother, Jane Thomas 42.

"'If we could just deal with this?"

"Very well," replied the Teacher. "How many days has he refused the data-dump?"

"Three."

"Three! Where is the male junior-adult now?"

39 knew he had to move fast. He grabbed a chair and jammed it under the handle.

Outside, 39 could see old Jones in the deepening twilight. He looked a bit like grandfather, but younger.

The key turned in the lock. 39's throat tightened with fear.

39 *had* to get away.

Like all junior-adults old enough to talk, 39 went with his preceding number to work as an assistant, taking a data-dump of information each day from his father's data-eye into his own. It was only at the office that the junior-adults could talk. Harry Thomas 34 had found a way to go beyond his father's memories, way back to Harry Thomas 1; that's how they found out about childhood.

39 had gone further still, beyond Peter Jones 1 to old Jones. He wasn't just a memory. In the twilight he was real.

The door opened and snagged on the chair.

"39! Open this door at once."

"No! Go away, Daddy!"

There was a shocked silence. *Daddy?* That was an ancient word—a word that called the dead to rise.

Outside the wind had risen. Leaves stirred as the trees shuffled and moved. Then the storm struck, bucketing down through the twilight.

Shapes formed and flashed in green. Sails and sunsets. Clawing hands. Briefly 39 saw a triple-Goddess—maiden, mother and crone. The maiden looked at him severely, while the crone leered. The mother was sad, and looked down at the lawn.

The shapes twisted again.

Old Jones raised his tree-wrought axe and mounted his green chariot. As the wind tossed the tree, old Jones rode his chariot. He stood tall and powerful, upright behind the horses like a god, his face alight with the glory of life. He flashed a smile at 39.

Old Jones was back!

39 reached out through his data-eye toward old Jones.

"Get me out of here!" pulsed 39 through the connection.

"Little Peter! Can you see my field of corn? Can you see my cattle upon the high pastures? I can sing you a song of battle, bloody and swift, amidst a storm's fury!"

39 groaned. Old Jones was always raving like this, but now he did not have the luxury of time.

"Listen! I have to get out of here!"

Old Jones raised his axe of wood and branches. Travelling on a gust, the mighty blades descended. The tree whipped down. The glass pane shattered, and old Jones extended his rough wooden hands through the window.

"39! Stop this!" yelled Peter Jones 38, his voice shrill with panic.

"Stand back, you fool," came the muffled voice of the Teacher through the door.

There was a crack as the Teacher's iron-rimmed boot heel hit the door. For one terrifying instant Peter 39 could see the iris of the Teacher's data-eye through the splintered door, fully open and dark with menace. Then the door smashed inwards, and the black-clad Teacher strode through the wreckage toward him, followed by his cowering parents.

39 grabbed old Jones's hand. The wind changed and the tree whipped back. Jones pulled him through the shattered pane, through the heavy rain and up into the canopy of his tree. 39 could see the shocked and fearful expressions of his father and mother, and the outrage of the Teacher. 39 met the Teacher's data-eye in triumph, then his heart went cold.

The Teacher smiled.

39 was drawn through the Teacher's data-eye, into the prison of his mind. His body went numb. Distantly he could feel the vice-like grip of the Teacher as he was hauled from the tree.

Everything around 39 was grey. He sat, naked and shivering, on the edge of a vast block of concrete which stretched out like a sea toward the horizon. The sky was bleak, and hovering in the place of the Sun was a massive eye, with a grey orb, black iris and even blacker pupil. Before him was a massive expanse, deepening below into the heart-emptying darkness of an abyss.

"Who else has been sharing eyes?!" thundered the eye. Its mouth opened shark-like, with rows of razor-sharp teeth ready to devour.

"No," whimpered 39. He was afraid, and wanted to protect his friends. Desperately he looked around for some escape. Hidden below the eye—in the deep murk of the chasm—was the entrance to a tunnel.

The eye slowly descended toward him. The iris grew . . .

In desperation 39 leapt off the edge of the concrete toward the tunnel opening. To his surprise, instead of falling, 39 shot straight for the opening like bullet.

"What are you doing?" said the eye, trembling with rage.

With a snarl the eye's mouth opened wide to snap at him as he passed, but missed him.

Then 39 was inside the tunnel.

The sky of grey was gone. In its place was a long chamber. 39

walked in wonder past murals and hieroglyphs, all dancing in the torchlight. Along one wall stood an endless series of elaborate wooden sarcophagi, each a little older than the next. They stretched back into the darkness like a silent army.

39 walked to the first one and threw it open.

Inside, was an ancient man, black-clad and corpse-like. The eye's opened and the man hissed, struggling through cobwebs to reach him.

The Teacher strode into the hall behind 39.

"What are you doing in here?!" yelled the Teacher.

The corpse-man shambled out of his standing coffin and pointed an accusing finger at the Teacher behind 39, "Charlie 63, how could you be so incompetent?" croaked the corpse-man.

"Charlie 62," mumbled the Teacher in shock. He turned toward 39, his face twisting in rage. "You are awakening my memories, you little bastard!"

39 knew where he was.

The Teacher's hands became steel razors, and he lunged for 39.

39 ran, deeper into the darkness, counting back the coffins until he reached the one he wanted, the last coffin. It was smaller than the rest, and made of plain grey-aged wood. He grabbed the lid and tried to move it.

"It won't budge!"

Desperately 39 looked around for some way to open it. Then he saw them. Rows upon row of nails, hammered into the lid like curses, sealing it shut.

"I have no idea how you learned to do this,"came the voice of the Teacher behind him, "but I have had enough of you mucking about in my mind, junior-adult."

Back in the brightly-lit entrance, Charlie 62 was still yelling. *"You are useless, 63. Useless! Do you hear me? You are a disgrace . . . "*

"Shut up, you old moron!" yelled the Teacher.

The Teacher raised his hands. The razor-sharp blades grew to the length of swords, "You will have no mind left, after I am finished with you, Peter Jones 39."

39 tried to run, but the Teacher's metal talons swept down, cutting off his retreat. 39 stagged away until his back was against the rough wood of the last coffin. *There was nowhere to run!*

The Teacher drew his hand back to strike; the glistening tips of the finger-swords poised at 39's eye-height.

Slowly, a single nail pushed itself from the coffin lid.

The Teacher saw the nail moving and froze. Transfixed, he watched the nail as it moaned its way out of the wood and chimed on the flagstones as it fell. One by one each of the nails pushed themselves from the box and tinkled to the floor. Then the coffin lid fell back.

Charlie 1 was a small man, balding and hunched with age. He wore a T-shirt, open at the neck, with plain suspender belts, and a set of pince-nez balanced beneath his enormous eyebrows. He walked briskly from the coffin and looked up at the Teacher over his pince-nez.

"What is going on here?" demanded Charlie.

The Teacher's face went white with fear.

"Answer me when I'm talking to you, young man. How dare you bring those weapons into my classroom! How dare you threaten a defenceless child!"

Seizing his chance, 39 dodged around the stunned Teacher and raced back up the hallway. Charlie 62, who was muttering and staggering around like a zombie, made a grab for 39, but he dodged past him with ease.

Young Peter, this way. It was the voice of old Jones!

The wall to 39's left opened onto a vast panorama of green. He leapt through the portal, back into his own mind.

The hall of memories and the Teacher were gone. Instead he was with old Jones in his chariot, galloping at breakneck speed across a wide and fertile plain. Wheat stretched out in wide furrows from the road.

Above, the hot sun beat down on a perfect, still day. The sky was a deep, endless blue.

"I am the Bear of the West!" yelled Jones to the winds. The team, a matched set of blacks, thundered on the road, and Peter looked up in admiration at Jones. His face was cleanly shaven, and he looked around twenty. Beneath his tartans his body was muscular, so unlike 38's.

"I have ridden this land since I was child," said Jones as he held the reigns of the chariot casually in his left hand.

"What is a child?" asked Peter.

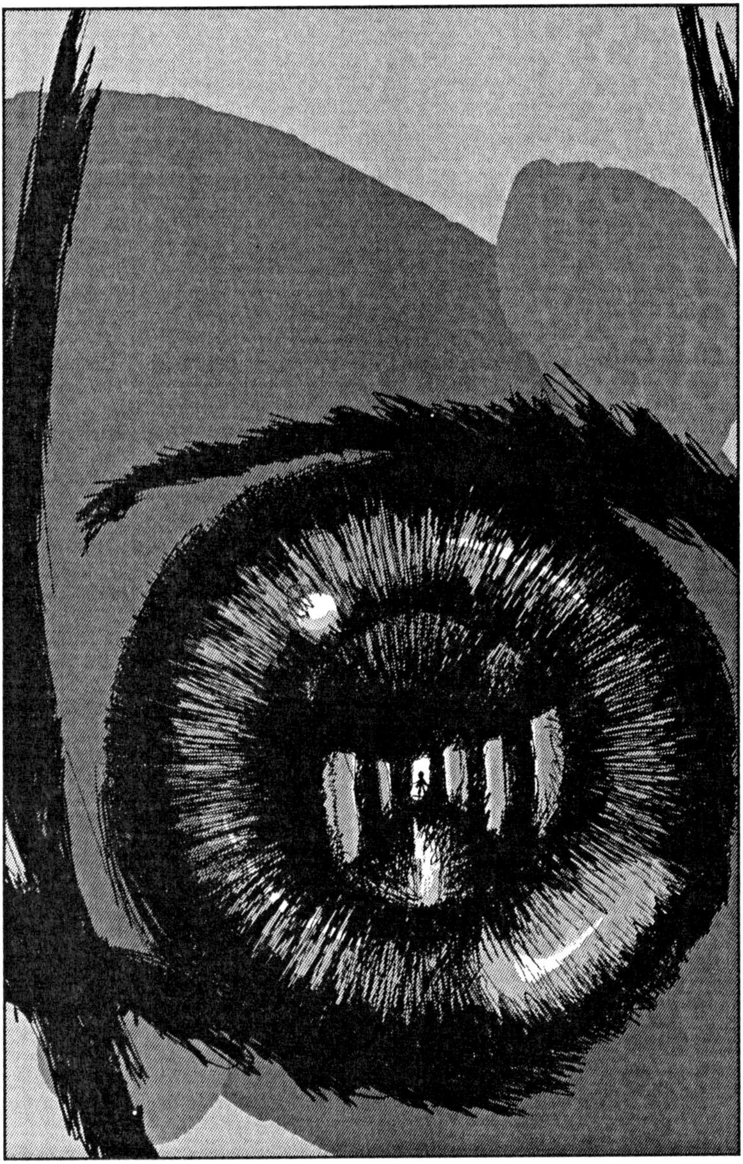

"You, a wee strap of a lad, need ask?"

The chariot sent sods flying as it turned and slowed.

"There is my dun," said Jones, pointing proudly to a wooden palisade on the hill. "The kingdom of youth. Do not let any gainsay it. For we are warrior-born and stride the world at twelve, ready for death. Maidens feel wise at fourteen and know their children may enter the Tree—themselves worn and in death by thirty. This is why you must cherish your youth, young Peter. This is why you must fight the Teacher, and carry the message to the others."

"How?"

Jones stopped the chariot.

"You have the strength, Peter," said old Jones, "Here," he said, offering him the reigns of the chariot. Ahead of him, a black-clad beast lumbered inexorably toward him. It was covered in decaying fur, its single eye huge and distended, hungry with teeth.

Peter gave a war cry and urged the chariot into motion. The blacks responded instantly, and the wind surged through his long hair. He felt the familiar grip of the long-handled axe in his hand and laughed. In front of him the eye-beast seemed impossibly slow.

The eye-beast turned to flee, but not quickly enough.

39's axe fell. It cleaved through the huge eye with ease. Rancid fluids splashed to the winds. The eye-beast gave a shudder then collapsed like a punctured balloon.

His mother screamed, and Peter found himself on the lawn below the tree. In front of him the Teacher sprawled unconscious.

"39, what have you done?"

"My name is Peter."

LES AUTRES
Adam Browne

At first, she was the opposite of an athlete.

Her name was Kimberley, but she was known as Kimba the White Line, for her devotion to powders. She was seeing a boy—called himself Jason Recliner—who spent his days getting stoned to the bone and staging VRex deathraces in a playscape fitted with massively parallel gore-engines (the closest, at that time, Kimba had come to any sort of sporting experience) . . . Still, she was happy. There was a chemistry between them.

Mainly consisting of the opiates they cooked up in their dinky little bioreactor.

With which they were forever playing, experimenting. Sussing out new formulas. Like the time they tried rustling up some mnemonics, but kept forgetting the recipe. Then there was the night they fluked a few micrograms of transcendorphin. At least they were pretty sure it was transcendorphin, sure enough to get all excited. (If heroin was a junkie, it would hit up transcendorphin to get stoned.)

But as it turned out, they were mistaken.

As it turned out, it was some nameless molecule, some fell chemical . . . And it killed Jason outright, and it chomped through her motor cortex until she was little more than a human tamagotchi . . . Uncomplicated little entity lying in ER going *beep!*—feed me; *wheep!*—clean me; *vlööp!vlööp!vlööp!*—replace my batteries (that was until the doctors adapted her life-support to run on the arterial turbines they'd seeded through her) . . .

Modern medicine had wrought the usual miracles: She could talk now, eat, breathe . . . But the bills were killing her. Especially crippling (not that she could be more crippled) were the payments on her smart armature—thing like some ironmaiden orthopaedic automaton swallowing her up flytrapwise. Clumsily, charmlessly, it helped her get places. Get nowhere.

She was alone now; very alone because around others she felt like a grotesque, a woebegone gork . . . She lived in a squat; an abandoned and heartbroken motor-home in the subsubbasement carpark of the derelict local mall.

A dark fungal place another writer might have peopled with fiends or fabulous beasts . . .

And then one night, while Kimba was dropping some old acid she'd found in her stash, a knock at the door. A visitor—which, for Kimba, was a beast as fabulous as any.

She was a woman so disabled that Kimba might have pitied her.

If not for her armature.

Fairytale dazzle of mother-of-pearl and father-of-diamond—chandelier poem cyberskeleton clockwalking her through the door with a scent of crystal.

"My name," she said, "is Marionette," flashing a creamy card: *National Institute of Sport*. "I am here to recruit you to our track and field team."

"This is a mistake—" Kimba began.

"*Paralympic* track and field, you understand."

"But look at me, I'm no more an athlete than you are . . . "

So the woman took hold of Kimba's chest brace. And nonchalantly lifted her into the air—the strength of her armature like something out of nightmare. "I am a weightlifter," Marionette said, perhaps unnecessarily, "classified Grade 1A paralympian with congenital degenerative quadriplegia." She twirled Kimba like a baton (the acid had kicked in, Kimba noted), tossed her tumbling up, caught her again with a flourish. "At last summer's games, I executed a lift of 567 kilos. Alas, a girl from the Chinese team lifted 570." She rolled Kimba into a ball and bounced her briskly on the floor. "But it was not her strength or talent that bested me. It was the strength and talent of her armature." She straightened Kimba into pencil-form (the trip shifting into higher gear) and sharpened her skull with a giant pencil sharpener. "Chinese sporting technology currently surpasses ours. But we're making great progress; perhaps soon our engineers will advance beyond theirs." She drew diagrams with the Kimba-pencil, illustrating her point. "And then we will win the gold."

"So," Kimba heard herself say, "you're looking for some addled spastic, some sorry-arsed cripple to wrap your machinery around?"

"Yes," Marionette replied, "and as such, you are eminently qualified."

"But why me, why this cripple in particular?"

"Because you can be bought." And then Marionette talked money, a language in which she was fluent—silky—voluptuous in her descriptions of training fees, per diems, annuities, stipends . . . Her words weaving in and out and through the acid and Kimba rising now on a great green wave of liquidity with fishsilver coins spinning and tumbling and shark shapes darking the deeps as she rose and rose in the wallowing welter.

Into the Paralympics Annex of the National Institute of Sport.

A louche blue cube on the city's outskirts.

The Biomechanics Studio at its heart. Loud machine-haunted space, greasy utilitarian bodyshop—like God's garage, Kimba thought as she clicketyclacked in her calipers past racks of surgical jackhammers and skullwrenches and prostheses flexing digital extremities . . . And the floor splashy with puddles of straw-coloured spinejuice, and nerve bundles slung fat and white over whatever was handy such as chair-backs and coat-racks and xylophonic bone-machines . . . And now a team of megageeks in grimy cleansuits helping her onto a table. Marvelling over the antiquity of her gear: "This life support needs life support . . . !" Straining at her superannuated bolts and connectors. Unpeeling the armature from her body—pleasure/pain of removing a scab—and discarding it on the floor. Where it twitched awhile, dreaming girlshell dying, and Kimba nakeder than she'd ever been. Her flesh with the pallor of some long-dead toxic mollusc, but with less appeal.

Now the upgrade.

They clad her in gold and kevlar and industrial diamond, in gossamer electrics and coppercoated cobwebs and polymerised coils of crystalline bliss—in Cinderella technoglitz as smart as arithmetic and as pretty as music. Machinery like sweet embrace. Factory fresh armature all suave around her with poise and soul-cool fluency as she rose from the table and was led flowing to a training hall.

Marionette was waiting.

"Your high jump sessions begin today," she said.

"High jump?" Kimba complained. "I don't know anything about high jump." Which was a lie because already she could feel the requisite knowledge informing her movements . . . Her machinery steeped in an athlete's calculus of ankle angles and flic-flac hip flip ballistics . . . The information kicking in like a craving, an addiction to something she'd never had. Now the high jump bar drawing her in for her first taste, and the run up like a dance; five long strides, then four more, faster, curving in on the bar. Then the parabolic up and over and she'd cleared three metres twenty as though she'd done it forever . . .

And the more she did it, the higher she got. Five metres. Seven. Day after day, higher and higher.

Until the morning she went for ten metres. Overleapt and cracked her skull on a roof beam. Died on the way down of massive brain trauma.

The armature continued the training for a week.

And no one realised what had happened until the corpse inside began to stink.

WAKE WHEN SOME VILE THING IS NEAR
Michael Kauffmann & Mark McLaughlin

Strother put a hand to his chest as he speedwalked to the bookstore. His heart was pounding like a drum—perhaps one of the sacred monastery drums from his novel. Today was the day. The day his book would hit the shelves at Wordplay, his favourite bookstore. The day his life would really and truly *begin*.

Wordplay was a chain store, but the management had given it a homey look by decorating the place with lace curtains, overstuffed couches and kitschy knick-knacks on little cherrywood tables. Toward the back there was a coffee shop, so the place always had that nutty, slightly spicy, fresh-roasted ambience. Strother bumped into a long-haired, round-bellied person on the way into the store. For a moment he thought it was a pregnant woman, and in a split-second of panic he worried that he might have harmed the baby. But then he saw the three-day stubble of the heavy-set young man.

"Watch where you're going, baldy," the man said.

"Sorry," Strother said, not wanting to make a fuss. Not on his special day. But still . . . *Baldy? I'm not that bald. I still have some left around the sides. Besides, I'm an author. A published author. I look distinguished.*

He rushed to the New Books table and looked up and down, left and right, trying to find his book. Then he realised the books were in alphabetical order by the author's name, so he found where the 'L' authors were located. Where was Lindstrom? He saw a book by someone named Lang. Next to it was a book by someone named

Lockwood.

His book wasn't there.

Then he realised: it had to be in the Local Interest section, since he was from the area. So he hurried to that section . . .

But his book wasn't there, either.

And it wasn't in General Fiction. Where was it? Where were they hiding it? It *had* been published, right?

Then he saw a sign that read HORROR in bright red letters. Of course. That's where it had to be. He crossed to those shelves and found the 'L' authors . . .

And there it was. One copy, spine facing the world, jammed in among dozens of other paperbacks. *The Yeti* by Strother Lindstrom. To its left was *Curse of the Man-Beast* by Stacy Kennedy. To the right, *Beware the Black Ice* by Ryan Masters.

Strother felt dizzy. He simply couldn't believe it. The books next to his first novel had major elements in common with it. His novel had a man-beast in it. And, his had ice in it—at least it wasn't *black* ice. And there was only one copy of his out, and several of the ones on either side.

He plucked his book off of the shelf. Maybe holding the book would cheer him up.

The cover was gorgeous: a huge, mega-hairy humanoid reaching out toward the reader from out of a snowbound mountain landscape. The creature had blood-red eyes, fat pink lips, black claws and a luxuriant pelt of shaggy white hair.

He turned the book over.

There was his author's photo. That was no surprise. He knew the publisher was going to use that photo—he'd sent it to them. But in comparison to the yeti on the cover, he looked like a shiny newborn babe.

He looked back toward the New Books table. Surely no one would mind if he put his book up there. It *was* new, after all.

On his way toward the front of the store, he passed a hardbound volume of Shakespeare with a scene from *A Midsummer Night's Dream* on the cover. He'd been in that play in college—he'd played Bottom, the villager who was given the head of an ass by the fairies. The papier mache head he'd worn had been covered with a layer of thick fake fur. The fairy queen, Titania, had been played by Suzie Molton, a girl he'd had a crush on for a couple years. Her character was supposed to fall in love with the ass-headed fool as soon as she opened her eyes. What was that one line—? Oh, yes. "Wake when some vile thing is near." In real life, she'd pretty much considered him a vile thing. She'd simply laughed when he asked her out.

She moved to Texas years ago, but he had heard she'd recently moved back to town. Perhaps someday she would come into the store and see the book.

He waited until no one was around, and then slipped up to the table and placed his book next to *Talons of Fate*, a best-selling political thriller about a fighter pilot. He looked at the author's picture on the back of the best-seller. That guy had plenty of thick, dark hair. He had more hair on his forearms than Strother had on his head.

"He'll be here later," said a perky voice behind him. He turned to face a chubby, middle-aged woman with a hairy mole on her chin. She wore a small badge that identified her as a manager. He couldn't recall ever seeing her before.

"Who?" Strother asked.

She tapped a copy of the thriller. "Prescott Sinclair. He'll be here to sign copies at two." She checked her watch. "Oh, that's only fifteen minutes away," she said as she shuffled off. "I'd better make sure everything's ready."

Strother went to the coffee shop for his usual: a low-fat, chocolate-cherry double latte with a dusting of nutmeg. Tony, the young man behind the counter, smiled at him. "Hi, Strother. Is your book out yet?"

"Yeah, but they only have one copy." Strother stuck out his bottom lip in a mock-pout. "I hear you've got some big-shot novelist coming in pretty soon for a signing. I wish they'd ask me to do a signing."

"Well then, talk to them," Tony said, flicking his long bangs out of his eyes. "Find the new manager and ask her. She has a big mole. Her name is Cheryl."

"I saw her a couple minutes ago." Strother thought for a moment. "Maybe I'll stick around for the signing and see if I can talk to her after it gets started."

Tony nodded. "That's the thing to do. You have to make things happen if you want to get ahead in life." He rolled his eyes. "Geez. Me, some coffee jockey, telling a published guy how to run his career."

"Oh, that's okay. Actually, your advice is right on the money."

They talked more as Strother drank his latte, and then another one. He was a little hungry, so he looked toward the lunch selections on display in the glass case to the side of the counter. He spotted the fuzzy hemisphere of a halved kiwi on a fruit plate and lost his appetite—even the produce here had full hair coverage.

Eventually he noticed that several people were flocking around one of the tables out in the central area of the bookstore. Apparently the big shot had arrived.

Strother said goodbye to Tony and moved closer to the action out on the floor. He had to admit that Prescott Sinclair was a really handsome guy, with boyish good looks and a mane of tousled brown hair. He seemed so confident, the way he smiled and chatted with all the fans, mostly women, jostling in front of his table. Strother hadn't realised that so many women read political thrillers. But then, with looks like that, Prescott could write a book about neutering pigs and ladies would still line up for miles to buy copies.

Strother saw the manager and walked up to her. "Hello again."

She looked at him and smiled. "Oh. Hello. Have we met?"

He sighed. Forgotten already. He wondered if he should even bother asking for his own signing session.

Then he saw, standing a few feet behind Prescott, the most unusual-looking man he'd ever seen in his life.

Not that the man was ugly . . . He was very tall and pale, with a wide face, wide set eyes and a broad, flat nose. He had a small, thin-lipped mouth and a pointed chin. But the strangest thing about him was his hair.

He had long, coiling hair that covered his shoulders and the upper half of his back. Most of the coils were golden-brown, while some were reddish and a few were dark auburn. The man was absent-mindedly chewing on the end of one of these coils.

"Wow. I've never seen hair like that before," he said, nodding toward the man.

The manager smiled. "Mr Vegarra. He's here with today's author."

"Really?" Were the two men brothers? Friends? Lovers? The long-haired man seemed to be watching the writer very closely.

"Mr Vegarra is his agent," the manager said. "He lives in town. I guess he decided to stop by to see how one of his meal tickets was doing. Now was there something you wanted me to help you with?"

Strother shrugged. "It's nothing. No big deal." He then wandered off—in the direction of the New Books. He grabbed the sole copy of his book and headed toward the agent.

What luck! Recently he had been wondering whether or not he should try to enlist an agent's services. His deal on his first book had been—Well, modest. He was now hard at work on his next book. In fact, he was about two-thirds done with it. Perhaps this longhaired fellow would be able to land him a great deal.

He walked up to the man, holding out the book. Before he could say one word, the man grabbed it from him.

"*The Yeti*," the man said in a loud, raspy voice. "Sorry, this ain't my life story! But I do look like the main character!" he said with a laugh that was more like a bray.

Where's the volume knob so I can turn this guy down? Strother wondered. "Actually, I wrote that book," he said. "The manager said you were an agent, so I thought I'd introduce myself. I'm Strother Lindstrom."

The man held out his free hand. "Raphael Vegarra."

Strother shook hands with him. The man's palm was very hot and uncomfortably damp. Strother caught a whiff of a sweet scent that seemed to be coming from—the agent? He couldn't quite identify it.

Vegarra did not immediately let go of his hand. Instead, he turned Strother's hand upward and looked at it. "Very good! Your fingers are all different lengths. Look how short your pinky is. That is the hand of a smart man."

"I didn't know that," the writer said. He'd always felt self-conscious about his short pinky. Granted, people didn't go around looking at each other's pinkies, but still, his was much shorter than most. In fact, he could twirl a pencil between his index, middle and ring fingers, and his little finger wouldn't even get in the way.

"Oh, yes. Men whose fingers are all the same length—I do not wish to call them stupid. Let us just say that their brains are not what they could be." The man grinned, and Strother was alarmed to see that his teeth were all very small and narrow, with spaces between them. What did *that* say about a man?

"Tell me what sort of deal you have with your current publisher," the agent said, glancing at the spine of *The Yeti*. "Largesse Press? I'm not familiar with them. Are they new? How are they promoting your book?"

As Strother answered the man's questions, he looked toward the autograph session. Some of the women were looking at Vegarra and a few were even looking at him. Yes, they no doubt could sense that the agent, though clearly eccentric, was a man of power, a mover-and-shaker. Perhaps they wondered if he, too, moved and shook.

"Can I keep this?" the agent said, holding up the book.

"Well, that's a store copy. I'd have to buy it for you—"

Vegarra laughed. "That's okay. I'll buy it on the way out. Do you want to have lunch this week sometime? How about the day after tomorrow?"

Strother put a hand to his chest. "Lunch? Sure! That would be great. What time is good for you?"

The hairy man tapped his forefinger on his chin. "Let me think ... I have that conference call at ten. Who knows how long that'll take? Then I'm going to an estate sale at two-thirty. How about this? Just stop by my place. Iris can whip us up something to eat, and we'll talk."

"I wouldn't want your wife to go to any trouble on my account. I can just pick up some sandwiches somewhere."

Vegarra's laughter brayed forth again. "Iris isn't my wife!"

Prescott stopped signing and turned toward them. "What? Did that guy think Iris was your wife?" He too laughed, and even shook his head in disbelief.

"Well, I've never met Iris ... " Strother chewed his lower lip. Had he said something wrong?

"Iris is quite a bit older than me. For all I know, she could be a thousand years old." The agent smiled. "Or maybe just five-hundred. She's an old teacher of mine who's staying at my place. Her husband died and she doesn't have anywhere else to go. A woman that age shouldn't have to live all by herself. She's a sweet old thing. She likes to show she's still useful. I'm sure she'd be happy to fix us something." He reached into his jacket and pulled out a bright yellow card. "Here's my address. See you at noon?"

"Sure." Strother looked at the card. The black lettering against the yellow paper reminded him of a bumblebee. 507 Winthrop Lane.

That was in the high-and-mighty west side of town, where all the rich folks lived. Bankers. Real estate Pooh-Bahs. Heart surgeons. Orthodontists. And apparently, literary agents.

•

Driving down Winthrop Lane in his old blue-edged-with-rust compact was a humbling experience for Strother. He felt fairly sure that in one of the many fine houses, some jewellery-strewn *grande dame* was looking out her bedroom window and crying to her butler, "Jeeves, alert security! There's a ramshackle car out on the street, bringing down property values. Have it destroyed immediately."

Of course, some rich people were nice. Vegarra was letting a lonely old widow stay with him. And he'd invited a struggling writer over for lunch.

On his way out of the store, Strother had looked for earlier books by Prescott Sinclair. He'd found only one—*Thunder Of Destiny*, another fighter-pilot epic, but from a much smaller press than his latest novel. This one had an author's picture on the back, too.

In this one, Prescott was very much bald.

Somewhere along the line, he'd have to find a way of bringing up that topic with Vegarra. If Prescott wore a hairpiece, maybe he needed to get one, too.

At last he found 507. The sight of it took his breath away. It was by far the fanciest house on Winthrop. No, not fancy: *stately* was the word. An enormous house—pillars and everything—bordered by rose bushes and statues of . . . What were those little mythological guys called? The ones with horns and goat-legs. The word escaped him.

He pulled up in front of the pink-and-grey marble steps that led to the enormous main entrance. He got out of the car and looked around, half-expecting a servant of some sort to come and park his vehicle. But one was not forthcoming, apparently. He walked up to the huge mahogany doors. He suddenly realised he was empty-handed. Should he have brought something? A little gift? A bottle of wine?

He rang the doorbell and waited. A minute passed. He looked around at the bushes, the lawn, trying not to look impatient, in case he was being watched by some surveillance camera. Maybe it was the old woman's duty to answer the door, and she was shuffling down some long hall at that very moment . . .

Suddenly the door swang soundlessly open. A tall, model-thin woman holding a martini glass answered the door.

"Sorry I took so long," she said. "Come in, darling." She had a low voice and a British accent. She looked to be about fifty, with fine-boned features and a bundle of blonde hair piled on top of her head and held in place with chopsticks and a thin black ribbon. "I told everybody I'd get the door, and then somebody started talking to me about—" She stared off into space for a few seconds. "—about something. It couldn't have been important. I've forgotten it already." She led him down a hall lined with portraits. Most of the people in the paintings bore some resemblance to Vegarra, and all had long, thick hair.

"Did you say 'everybody' . . . ?" Strother asked.

"Oh, you don't know. Of course not, how could you?" The woman smiled. "You know about Iris, right? Well, she can be a little *over-enthusiastic*. He'd asked her to make a little something for lunch—for just you two—and for some reason she whipped up a regular banquet. She really went to a lot of trouble. So he made a few calls and invited some of us over to eat it all."

"That was nice of him," he said.

"I'm Claudia, by the way," the woman said.

"I'm—"

She laughed. "I know who you are, darling."

"Oh."

She swirled her drink in its glass. "Vanilla vodka. Want some?"

He shook his head. "I've never tried it, but—" He suddenly realised: he couldn't say it was too early in the day for such a drink. Evidently *she* didn't think so. "—but I'm not much of a drinker."

They soon arrived in the dining room. Claudia was right: the old woman had prepared a feast suitable for a family reunion. Two tables were covered with dishes—sliced roast beef, a tray of julienned vegetables, roasted new potatoes, and much more. The whole room smelled of roast meat and another, subtle sweet scent.

Vegarra stood by a huge bay window, talking with a group of six people. He waved and walked over. "Strother! So glad you could make it. I trust Claudia has told you about Iris' cooking marathon? Our little lunch has turned into a full-blown banquet, I'm afraid."

"That's okay." He looked around the room. "Which one is Iris?"

"Why, here she comes now." Vegarra pointed toward the room's entrance.

Strother turned, and had to bite his tongue to keep from crying out. Iris was, in a word—hideous.

The old woman was hugely fat, with coarse, wrinkled skin and huge, dark bags under her eyes. Her lips were thick and blubbery and her cheeks were networked with broken veins. Her long white hair was woven into two thick, sloppy braids, draped over her shoulders. She wore a white dress with a flowing scarf dotted with a pattern of daisies. Her arms had a lot of drooping chicken-skin on them, but a lot of muscle, too. For someone who looked old enough to have once dated a Pharaoh, she seemed extremely powerful, and she moved quickly. She practically skipped over to them.

"Who is this boy, this baby boy? Our special guest?" she said in a high, nasal voice, in an accent Strother couldn't place. *To her I must seem like a baby*, he thought.

"Yes, Iris. This is Strother Lindstrom," Vegarra said.

"My Raphael, he finds the idea of working with you very exciting," the old woman said, grabbing the writer by the hand. "I am Iris Grell. Come with Auntie Iris, let me fix a nice plate for you."

So saying, she pulled him toward the food table.

"I love your new book," she said, matter-of-factly. "Quite an adventure. I read it at one sitting, which is unusual for me. At my age, I am bored with everything. You did a marvellous job. But such a small publisher! I told Raphael, 'My lamb, you must help this baby boy. Make a rich big-shot out of him, please.' Would you like that?" She shoved a plate into his hands.

"Of course!" He watched as the old woman piled way too much food on his plate. "Thank you for putting in a good word for me like that. I mean, we don't even know each other, and—"

"Soon, we shall be the best of friends. I am sure of it." She filled a plate for herself. "Ah, Raphael is talking with Claudia. Let's you and I sit and eat, and let the lovebirds coo." She nodded toward a table.

"Is Claudia his girlfriend?"

"Just a client—for now! A man should not be alone for too long. They have their needs, as I'm sure you know." She gave him a smile that looked more like a grimace. "Are you enjoying the rhubarb mousse? It is my own special recipe."

Strother was in the middle of a mouthful of the mousse, and indeed, he was not enjoying it. He was in fact repulsed by it. It felt like it had a hair or two in it—he could feel something on his tongue, horrible and wiry. But perhaps it was just the fibres from the rhubarb stems. He managed to choke down the disturbing mess. "Oh, yes, delicious," he said. *I think I'm going to faint*, he thought.

Iris glanced back toward the table. "What a pity. No more mousse left. The others have gobbled it up. These are clients of my wonderful Raphael—the ones who live in the area. He has so many clients. He is such a genius. He was made them all rich, and he will do the same for you." She looked around the room. "Ah, I see he and Claudia have left together. Wonderful."

Strother gasped. "He's gone?"

Iris waved her hand dismissively. "Not to worry. Talking to me is like talking to him. If I think it's a good idea, so will he." She suddenly thrust the fingers of her right hand between her breasts and pulled a little white stick out of her cleavage.

My God, a reefer, Strother thought.

The old woman grimace-smiled again. "You should see the look on your face, my baby boy. Do you think this is one of those marijuana joints the naughty teenagers smoke? Have no fear. This is just a cigarette, hand-rolled by my own dainty fingers, using a Belgian blend of tobacco that I have shipped to me. The store cigarettes, they are like poison. This, on the other hand, is heaven. But legal, my friend. Completely legal. And flavoured with vanilla." She then pulled a lighter out of her cleavage.

Strother, realising that he was staring at her enormous breasts, looked away. *Good Lord, what else does she have down there?*

She then lit up, and the stench of the blend made Strother want to gag. The smoke smelled like a sickly combination of candy, burning hair and sour milk.

"Now let us talk about your future," the old woman said. "I see great things ahead for you, my baby boy."

•

A week later, at the bookstore, Strother ordered a vanilla latte and told Tony about his visit to 507 Winthrop Lane.

"I've been there three times since then," the writer said as he sat nursing his drink, "and I only ever talk to Iris. Raphael is always on his way somewhere with Claudia. She's one of his clients. She's doing a signing here today—her new book just came out. Anyway, I guess that old woman pretty much rules the roost. She's always there, smoking those vanilla cigarettes."

"You must like the smell of them," Tony said. "You've never ordered a vanilla latte before."

"Really?" the writer looked at his cup. "I guess you're right. It's not a bad smell, really. I didn't like it at first, but I'm getting used to it."

"A person can get used to anything, I suppose. Hey, what's this?" Tony reached toward Strother's head.

The writer pulled back. "What are you doing?"

Tony laughed. "I was going to rub that fuzz of yours. Looks like cat fur—never seen that before. Are you taking that hair-growing stuff? That stuff on those commercials? Come on, you can tell me."

Strother ran his hands over his scalp. It wasn't as smooth as usual—there seemed to be a light layer of stubble. He sprang to his feet and ran toward the men's room.

Once inside, he bounded up to the mirror over the sink. His heart pounded furiously. Yes! New hair was coming in! And he wasn't even doing anything to make it happen. Over the years he'd tried creams, lotions, special caps, with no results. Now it was coming in all by itself.

He smiled joyously at his reflection. Hair! Maybe someday he'd have lots of long hair—thick, shining hair—like Vegarra. Or Claudia. Or Iris . . .

He watched his smile in the mirror slowly fade away. Funny, that he should be growing this new hair after joining this new group of friends. All of them had long hair . . .

Lots and lots of it.

He closed his eyes and shook his head. *Snap out of it. This isn't something freaky. Women who hang out together start having their periods at the same time. Maybe this is something like that. My scalp's playing follow the leader. That's all.*

He licked his lips and tasted vanilla.

He went back out into the bookstore. Vegarra and Claudia had arrived, and Cheryl was chatting with them as she prepared a table for the signing. He waved and walked over to them.

"Darling!" Claudia gushed. "So good of you to attend my little fanfest. Of course, now that you're part of our scene, you'll be having signings when your new book hits the stands. Signings all over the country."

Strother put a hand to his chest. "Really?" He looked down at the dust jacket of one of the hardcovers on the table—*Beverly Hills Bedrooms*, by Claudia W. Rothschild. He wondered if he should start using a middle initial. It seemed so classy.

Vegarra nodded. "Signings are a vital part of the whole process. And I do like to start the signing tours right here, at my very favourite bookstore. Right now, Prescott is off travelling from state to state, meeting all his old fans, making new fans . . . "

"Yes, generating interest. Energy. Excitement." Claudia gave Strother a slow, knowing wink.

"Wow. It all sounds so *glam*," Cheryl said.

Vegarra rested his hand on the manager's shoulder. "My dear, you don't know the half of it."

•

Four months later, Strother presented the finished manuscript for his new book, *Howl For A Blood-Red Moon*, to Iris.

They were having a picnic on the lawn of 507 Winthrop Lane. The two of them sat on a chequered sheet amidst numerous plates and bowls. The shadow of one of the goat-legged statue-men fell squarely across a plate of rhubarb mousse. Strother spooned up his third helping.

Iris ran her pudgy fingers through his thick golden-brown hair. "I am so happy to see you have a healthy appetite," she said. "So many people these days, they see all the skinny actors on TV, and they say, 'Oh, I must be skinny, too, or else no one will want to go to bed with me!' Ha! Fat people enjoy the pleasures of the flesh, too. They have so much more flesh to pleasure!"

Strother nodded. A few thin strands contained in the mousse dangled from his smile, but he sucked them right up. "So have you and Raphael figured out which publisher would be best for my new book?"

"Not just yet. But rest assured, we will land you a peach of a deal," the old woman said. "Raphael is highly regarded. He knows quality when he sees it. As do I." She chewed on the very tip of one of her braids.

"But neither of you has read my new book yet." He tapped the top page of the manuscript. "I've only just finished it. Maybe it needs a lot of editing. Maybe it isn't very good."

Iris clucked her tongue. "My little pink piglet, still you wallow in self-doubt! We have read your first book. It is too marvellous for words. We are experienced in these matters." She stood up and held out her hand. "Trust us without question."

Strother took her hand and stood beside her. He looked down at his manuscript and bent to pick it up.

"Leave it," the old woman said. "No one is going to steal it."

Iris then led him to the house—but not to the front. She led him to a small side door behind a row of rose bushes. A small bronze mask was mounted in the middle of the door. The metal face had angular features, pointed teeth and small, rounded horns.

Iris reached into her cleavage and pulled out a bronze key.

She unlocked the door and walked inside, and Strother followed.

He found himself in what appeared to be a large chapel. In the centre was a small stage, bordered on all sides by seven rows of chairs. On the stage was one of the goat-man statues, surrounded by seven censers hanging from bronze chains. A foul, musky reek filled in the air.

This indoor statue was very different from the rest. It was twice as large, and covered with black, matted hair. It had a thick mane of long, curling locks. And the face was that of Raphael Vegarra.

"That smell," Iris said, shaking her head. "Hard to get used to, even after all these years." She took her lighter from her cleavage and lit the censers, one by one. "But we have found that vanilla masks the odour quite well. Vanilla. So sweet and innocent. And still the most popular flavour for ice cream, I believe."

Strother noticed that the walls of the chapel were lined with bookshelves. The room contained thousands of books—some appeared to be huge, leather-bound and probably extremely old.

When she finished lighting the censers, Iris went to a corner of the stage and pulled a velvet rope that hung from the shadows overhead. Somewhere in the house, a bell rang. She then returned to the statue and pulled off a tuft of its fur.

She popped it into her mouth and began to chew.

From the back of the chapel came the creak of a door opening. Soon Vegarra, Claudia and Prescott Sinclair walked onto the stage.

The agent took his hand. "Strother, I'm so sorry I haven't been able to spend more time with you lately. Claudia and I are going to be married, and we've been busy with all sorts of preparations. I trust Iris has been looking after you?"

Claudia and Prescott walked up to the statue and, like Iris, gobbled down tufts of hair.

Claudia turned to Strother. "You really must have some," she said. "Like so many things, it tastes better than it smells."

"Try the hair from the head," Vegarra whispered to Strother. "It's longer and thicker. It's the secret ingredient in Iris' mousse."

Strother put a hand to his chest. He knew he should be repulsed by these loathsome people and their vile ways. But he also knew that he was still hungry, and that only one thing would satisfy that hunger—

The statue's longer locks, he found, were indeed delicious. They tasted like a deliciously impossible combination of roast lamb and dark chocolate. And it wasn't dry at all, as one might expect hair to be. It slid easily down his throat. His fingers and toes were beginning to tingle.

"Careful, do not eat too much," Iris said. "It is a delicacy, and one does not gobble down delicacies. Besides, too much is . . . not good for you. Or perhaps I should say, it is too good for you."

Strother paused in his feasting, his chin lightly bearded with overflow from his mouth. "How will I know when I've had too much?"

The others exchanged glances—he wasn't quite sure whether they were amused or worried by his question. Finally Vegarra said, "Iris is being overly cautious. *Anything* in extreme excess is bad for you—even water or oxygen. Just eat. Enjoy."

As Strother ate, he wondered about the books. "Those really old books must be interesting. Can I look at your collection later?"

"Of course," Iris said. "I will show you some volumes, many centuries old, that I'm sure you will find enlightening. It is time for you to learn more about our . . . little family. The Way of the Page."

"The Way of the Page." Strother repeated, smiling. Now his whole body felt like it was tingling. He felt like something marvellous was happening to him. Something sexual and religious and ancient and yet altogether new.

"Yes, darling. We have churches all over the world," Claudia said. "And the funny thing is, they don't even know they're our churches."

"Oh?" Strother plucked some eyebrow hairs off of the statue. "So what do they think they are?"

"Bookstores," Vegarra said. "What else?"

•

One day, while he was shopping at the mall, Strother happened to see Suzie Molton standing by the window of a tobacco shop.

He was amazed—not because she had improved with age, but because, well, she'd gone to hell. She still had curly blonde hair, but while she had once been fair-skinned and fine-boned, she was now leather-faced and scarecrow-skinny. He recalled that she'd been a heavy smoker and a real party-girl. Evidently years of Texas sun, unfiltered cigarettes and hangovers weren't much of a beauty treatment.

"Hi, Suzie," he said. "Remember me?"

She stared at him. "Um . . . Strother? Is that you?" Her eyes moved up a notch, directing her stare at his hair.

"Yes, I'm me," he said, smiling. "How are you doing?"

She opened her mouth, closed it, opened it again—apparently the question didn't have an easy answer. At last she said, "Okay. Hey, I ran into your cousin Jimmy the other day. He said you wrote a book."

"Yes, and it was published. And my new agent is getting me an even better deal on my next one." He found himself nodding, and stopped. No need to show her how much he enjoyed putting her in her place.

"You're really doing great. I—" She cocked her head to one side. "I haven't been having much luck. My husband died a few years back. Then I had some problems with my back and I was off work for a long time. But I don't want to bore you with all that crap. Do you want to go get a drink somewhere?"

Strother shrugged. "Why not? How about that Mexican place by the shoe store?"

Her over-tweezed eyebrows shot up. "Margaritas? Sure!"

He *so* wanted to tell her about the Way of the Page, just to scare her, but as they walked, he decided it would be best just to *show* her. He looked forward to experiencing that tingling again. He loved that feeling. Iris said that particular sensation meant that their god, He Who Instructs, was truly pleased.

Five margaritas later—one for him and four for Suzie—he suggested that they take a little drive out into the country. On the way out of the mall, they stopped in a liquor store and bought some tequila.

In a secluded, tree-lined lane, Suzie passed out long before they reached the worm at the bottom of the bottle.

Her hair tasted good, but the tingling, sadly, was pretty weak. Probably because her hair was over-processed. He carried her into the nearby woods, leaned her against a tree and poured the rest of the tequila all over her. He set her purse in her lap. He took her make-up mirror out of the purse and placed it in her hand.

Ah, the poor booze-addled hag. Truly she would see a vile thing when she woke up.

•

Iris gave Strother hair from the statue whenever he came by to visit. She told him fascinating stories about He Who Instructs. Some people called him Pan, while others mistakenly called him the Devil. Would the Devil be such a loving benefactor? The statue wasn't the actual god. It was simply a present from him—a gift that kept on giving.

"Our horned friend is a misunderstood fellow," she said one day. "Really, he only wants to share his knowledge with his chosen ones. In time, he will visit you in dreams, and perhaps you will put some of his knowledge in your books. We will change the world one page at a time."

Strother made nocturnal visits to the dumpster behind a hair salon near his home—there was always plenty of hair in there. He also started looking in dumpsters and trash cans from other salons. He didn't tell Iris how much hair he was eating—it wasn't her concern anyway. His new menu wasn't hurting anybody. Well, perhaps it had upset Suzie, but she'd deserved it. And after all, it would grow back.

Plus, he had lost a few pounds! Why not? His diet had a lot more fibre in it now. And best of all, he had more hair than ever. He had a thick mane that was almost as long as Vegarra's. He had to shave three times a day. And his back, chest, arms and legs were all covered with a thick, warm layer of fur, just like the yeti in his first book. But he had to wear long-sleeved shirts all the time, because people just wouldn't understand.

•

At last came the day of Strother's first signing at Wordplay. His new book had hit the shelves. This—yes, this was when his life would really and truly begin.

Iris even showed up for the event, wearing a long purple dress and a yellow scarf. "My button-eyed puppy," she whispered in his ear, "I am so very proud of you! Tomorrow I will give you your schedule for your next dozen signings. You must go out and dazzle the world—for me, for Raphael, and for the Way of the Page." She leaned toward him and sniffed. "Ah! You are wearing the cologne I gave you. My favourite scent."

Strother looked hungrily at her long hair. "Did you bring something for me to eat?" He'd had a big bowl of hair for breakfast that morning, taken from a salon dumpster the night before. But still he wanted more.

She nodded. "But of course!" She reached into her purse and pulled out a sandwich wrapped in wax paper. "It has plenty of my special ingredient in it."

He pouted. "Is that all?"

"You want more? That is surprising." Her thick eyebrows lowered in a worried glance. "How much hair are you eating these days? More than I know about, perhaps? Maybe you shouldn't have this—"

Cheryl hurried up to them, and Iris moved away. But Strother quickly snatched the sandwich from her before she was out of reach.

"Wow, you must be hungry," the manager said as the writer tore open the wax paper. "There are some cookies back in the employee lounge."

"No, this will be fine, thank you," Strother said around a mouthful of the sandwich. He stared at the hairs on Cheryl's mole.

"The table's all ready, so if you'll take your seat, we'll begin."

As Strother began signing books for customers, he noticed that Iris was talking with Vegarra near the magazine section. Iris had a worried, almost frantic expression, and they both kept looking his way.

He signed a book for a woman with long, brown hair. He signed one for a young man with thick red hair. Red hair! That was especially tasty. Then he signed one for an old man with dark, salt-and-pepper hair. He kept signing and looking at hair. Looking at hair. Looking at everyone's wonderful, delicious hair.

Then a young man with long, thick black hair walked up to him. "Could you sign it, 'Happy Holidays, Julianne'? I'm going to give it to my sister when Christmas rolls around."

Strother nodded. "Is your sister's hair as long as yours? As black as yours?"

The young man stared at him. "Why do you want to know?"

The author grinned. "Lean forward, please. I want you to check to be sure I spelled your sister's name right."

"Oh. Okay." He leaned forward and—

Strother yanked out a lock of the man's hair.

The next few minutes went by in a mad, tingling blur. Strother found himself shoving handfuls of hair into his mouth, faster and faster. Yellow hair, red hair, brown hair, black hair—all the hair he could grab. Folks were screaming, but what did it matter? Iris yelled, "No! Stop, my baby boy!"—but there was no way in the world he could stop. His entire body was tingling wonderfully. People tried to hold him down, but they went away yowling after he pulled out some of their hair. Even Vegarra tried to stop him, so he started ripping out the agent's hair—that was the tastiest of all.

As he ate he realised, to his frustration, that it was becoming more difficult to grip and pull at the hair. His arms and legs seemed to be growing numb, and he was having trouble controlling his movements. He reached out for another delicious handful of Vegarra's hair, but his fingers flopped uselessly against the agent's head.

People throughout the store were shouting things like "crazy man" and "call the police." Then Iris cried, "No! Oh, no! You must stop! *What have you done to yourself?*" Soon she was sobbing.

The tingling reached a level of unspeakable ecstasy—that soon

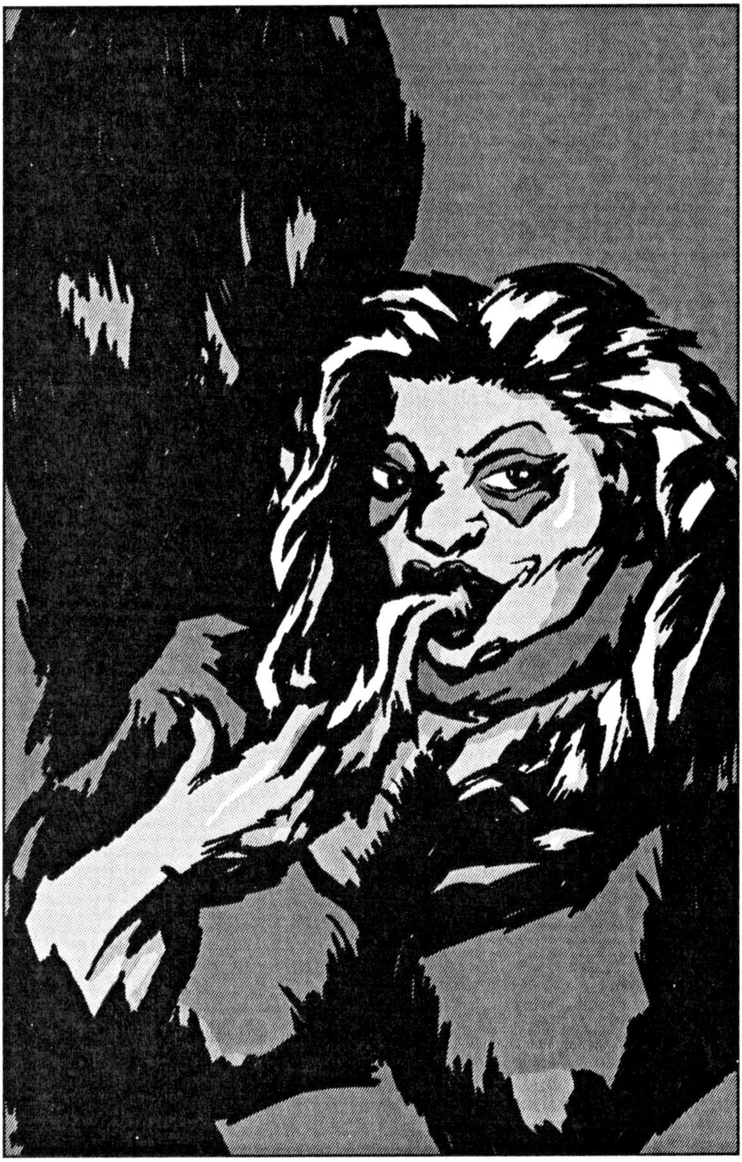

gave way to soul-shredding torment.

At that point he did indeed stop, and weakly put a hand to his chest. His fingers twitched and then began to *unravel*. Each one was dividing into countless twisting filaments. *Oh no*, he thought madly, *I'm getting split-ends*. The skin on his hands and arms began to transform into thick locks of multi-coloured hair. *I'm the vile one after all*, his mind sobbed, just before it lost the ability to comprehend words.

Then all of his muscles and organs, even his bones broke down into a growing, swirling, shining mass of hair, more luxuriant than that of any yeti.

THE WRONG STUFF
David McAlinden

A moonrocket is not the usual means of stabbing somebody to death. The usual tool is a kitchen knife, because most killings are domestics. To the best of my knowledge, a Saturn 5 moonrocket has never been used to dispatch a single victim, let alone hundreds of them. Not until I started, anyway.

EarthNetGlobal . . . 02/25/08/1634EST . . . Channel 5 . . . CONTACT FROM ANOTHER WORLD . . . WE ARE NOT ALONE . . . Alien starship approaching Earth. Arecibo takes the first call. Defence forces on full alert. Hubble repositioned. We go live to Channel 1 . . .

There were 3 stages to a Saturn 5 rocket. The S-IC (first stage) had five F1 engines that delivered a total thrust of 33 meganewtons. The S-II (second stage) and S-IVB (third stage) used J2 engines, five on the S-II and one on the S-IVB. The last Saturn 5 to stand on the launchpad was 110.64 metres tall, the titanium 1:400 scale model that I am stabbing repeatedly into Bill Simpson's flabby neck is 27.5 centimetres tall when standing upright on my desk. The real Saturn 5 weighed over 2700 tonnes in launch configuration. I'm not sure how much my model weighs, I wonder if Bill does. Crimson comets of blood spray out of the puncture wounds in his neck, their elliptical orbit ensuring an inevitable collision with me, the carpet, the walls, the chair he is sagging in, and the photomosaic of Mars on his desk.

EathNetGlobal . . . 02/26/08/0837EST . . . Channel 5 . . . I COME IN PEACE, SAYS ALIEN . . . Arecibo starts receiving data from the starship . . . sole occupant is ambassador from Enkassa, the alien home planet . . . Earth invited to join the Enkassan Federation . . .

A grey world enlivened by contact from the stars. Outside, the rain falls in hard metallic sheets, ricocheting from the flat planes and sharp angles of buildings, but slicing through those not protected. Inside, it is warm gloomy and stinking. I don't know if I'm in a bar or at a party. People of all size, shape and desirability are drinking and talking, their voices merging to form a continuous wave of white noise. Live feed from Hubble's telecam of the alien ship flickers on the TV. The commentator is babbling self importantly—ludicrously so to my ears—about how we can benefit from joining the Enkassan Federation, improve our technology and accelerate mankind's inevitable colonisation of the solar system. I know that this concept excites many people, but the thought of humans spiralling out from Earth and spreading like a plague through the galaxy makes me feel disconnected and homicidal. I imagine my Saturn 5 launching into a clear blue sky and embedding itself in a chest cavity.

EarthNetScience . . . 02/28/08/1300EST . . . Channel 9 . . . DISSEMINATION OF DATA DOWNLOAD FROM ENKASSAN STARSHIP . . . Enkassa is an earth-sized rocky planet (key +2 for pix). Thirty per cent of the planet is habitable landmass, with the carbon-based Enkassans being the dominant species. Photosynthesising woody plants are abundant and home to mammalian, reptilian and insectoid species. The remaining seventy percent of the planet is covered in water. There are no ice caps and the atmosphere, although similar to Earth, is warmer by an average 8 degrees Celsius. Enkassa orbits Phelbia, a gas giant three times the mass of Jupiter. Phelbia in turn orbits the parent star—known to us as Upsilon Andromedae—which is 44 light years from our own sun. The planet we now know as Phelbia and two other gas giants were discovered orbiting Upsilon Andromedae in 1988 by San Francisco State University astronomers Geoffrey Mason and R. Paul Butler, using Doppler spectroscopy data analysis. Following this discovery, Upsilon Andromedae became a shortlisted target for the Terrestrial Planet Finder, due for launch in August 2009 . . .

I loved my sister dearly, but now she is dead. Her parents—I don't think of them as mine anymore—had inexorably converted her into something that evolution had not planned, a stultification of all her promise. After converting my sister, they tried to do the same to me. They achieved success, but not in the way they imagined. I saw my sister three days before she died. She was only twenty seven, yet looked fifty—her blonde hair falling out, the green blue eyes I remembered now a dull and sightless grey, her gentle, lilting voice compressed to a croaking monotone, her body horribly emaciated. She no longer possessed the strength to purge her stomach of the food that was being forced into it, but by then it didn't really matter. A year after my sister's funeral, the thing I used to know as father had choked on his own blood trying to protect the thing I knew as mother. I killed her next and then burned down the house I used to know as home. These were the first humans I ever killed. Previously, I had killed only animals—cats and dogs mainly.

EarthNetScience . . . 03/12/08/2200EST . . . Channel 9 . . . FRUSTRATION AS ENKASSAN AMBASSADOR REFUSES TO DIVULGE SECRET OF FASTER THAN LIGHT TRAVEL . . . *all we know is this—the Enkassan ambassador has advised that the journey from Enkassa to Earth took three days and speculation is rife as to how this was achieved . . .*

Eating at Walt Shelby's place is essential, but dull. I sit in his hideously decorated dining room; elegantly forking overcooked vegetables into my mouth. The wine is an excellent Zinfandel, although I suspect the Shelbys purchased it because of the pretty label. Mrs Shelby—clueless, badly made up and drunk—is yacking loudly about some new shrubs she has purchased from Wal Mart.

" . . . and then they suggested I try the holly, but I didn't really want holly, but they said it'd complement the picket fence, but the spines, I said . . . "

"Holly is fashionable in Europe, Mrs Shelby, but I'd have suggested *Prunus lusitanica* instead, far better suited to Florida and it would really complement your architecture. It has these dark green leaves that suggest real permanence . . . " I trail off, suppressing a giggle as Walt unsuccessfully chases a rogue potato around his plate. He is studiously ignoring his drunken wife, trying to hide the fact that he hates her even more than I do. Mrs Shelby stares at me with a glazed intensity, her expression one of horticultural adoration.

" . . . why don't I drive you to that plant centre up on Kingswood this afternoon, Mrs Shelby? It'd give me great pleasure to find *Prunus lusitanica* for you." Actually, it would give me even greater pleasure to hack off Mrs Shelby's head with Walt's axe, so why the fuck did I make such a dumb timewasting offer? As penance for being stupid—discipline is paramount—I stab my right thigh quite hard with my food fork, unseen by the perfect couple. Waiting for the pain to subside, I gaze through the solarized windows at the white picket fence, glinting imperiously in the bright sunshine. Cocooned within its protective embrace is the neat garden, consisting of artificially green lawn, antiseptic soil and manicured shrubs. Upon the smooth asphalt driveway sits Mrs Shelby's BMW, haphazardly parked with the drunken insouciance of the chronic alcoholic. Feeling physically sick, I imagine stabbing Mrs Shelby with my Saturn 5. The sickness subsides, but a headache is looming, expanding, filling my brain, not with the instantaneous violence of a supernova, but with the measured aeonic pace of a swelling red giant. As my brain pushes against its meninges, I experience a temporal shift. With seamless precision, the BMW transmogrifies into a pockmarked red rock. The rest of this soulless suburban scene—the clean concrete road, the faux antique streetlamps, the swimming pools, the orderly timber framed houses, the neat eucalyptus trees, the neighbour polishing his Bentley—dissolves into a rusty red plain. All external noises—Mrs Shelby's tiresome drone, the clatter of cutlery on china plates, the air conditioning, the ice machine—fade out, to be replaced with the soft moan of a musical wind.

EarthNetGlobal . . . 03/25/08/0800EST . . . Channel 5 . . . DOUBLE FIRST . . . PARKER TO VISIT ENKASSA . . . *first man on Mars (key + 6 for library pix) chosen as Earth ambassador to Enkassa. Mars hero Colonel Jackson G. Parker unanimously appointed by UN Space Council to accompany the Enkassan ambassador to her home planet. NASA administrator Walton B. Shelby said : "Jack Parker is a hero to me—I cried when I saw him walk on Mars. He is uniquely qualified to undertake this mission." Colonel Parker is not your average astronaut—and your average astronaut is anything but average. A former combat pilot, he has degrees in biology, geology and astronomy. On 25 December 2005, he became the first human to set foot on Mars after a nine-month voyage on the USS Wells. Since returning from Mars, Colonel Parker has selflessly used his fame to help raise millions of dollars for charity . . .*

EarthNetScience . . . 03/27/08/1200EST . . . Channel 9 . . . SIMPSON'S DREAM TO BECOME A REALITY—SUPER PLANTS WILL COLONISE MARS . . . Amery Ice Shelf, Antarctica . . . Scientists at the Simpson Corporation's PhotoGene Research Station are now convinced that the so called Black Rainbow plants will survive and thrive on Mars. Bill Simpson's dream—to seed Mars with climate changing plants—now seems close to a reality. Head of PGRS Professor Don McKinsey predicts that within the year Black Rainbow will be en route to Mars. "We've spent the last two years developing Black Rainbow and demonstrating that it can survive in a simulated Martian environment," said McKinsey. "Now we're almost ready to begin the mission of the century—to send Black Rainbow to Mars and so begin the process of terraforming the Red Planet. This was Bill Simpson's dream and a habitable Mars will one day be his legacy to the world." The brutal murder of Simpson last October remains unsolved . . .

I watch the President on TV, talking to the alien on a giant com screen. I don't know what either of them is saying because the sound is turned down. The Prez looks like he is trying to lip-synch to Tom Jones blasting from my speakers. Maybe he is, maybe he's a Tom Jones fan and connected to me somehow. The Prez looks good, but he's full of shit, everyone knows it, but nobody cares. I don't know if the Enkassan girl has the hots for him, but she sure is smiling. Or maybe it's a grimace—hard to tell with these funny lips. Maybe he repels her. Maybe she thinks her planet has made a big mistake contacting Earth—let's try again in one thousand years, assuming the morons don't annihilate themselves in the meantime.

Giggling, I ask my companion if the Prez makes her horny like I know Tom Jones does. She doesn't answer. My anger fires up, there is a chainsaw screaming at full power in my head, the ceiling and floor begin advancing towards each other, compressing the walls and the TV screen, distorting the face of the Prez, causing his mouth to swallow his head and making him seem more alien than the alien. Then it all stops, as I remember that I stabbed my companion to death a few hours ago. That would explain her rudeness. I feel more conciliatory then.

EarthNetGlobal . . . 03/29/08/2230EST . . . Channel 5 . . . FBI INVESTIGATES THREAT TO KILL PARKER . . . Ambassador Parker, currently preparing for Enkassan trip, receives death threat from religious fundamentalists opposed to alien contact. "Listen, I'm religious too—I'm a Catholic—but I'm going for all of humanity," said

Parker. The FBI refused to confirm or deny a possible link between this threat and the Bill Simpson killing . . .

I walk into the office. There is a tall guy standing at my desk, his back to me, staring at a wall mounted photomosaic of Mars. He senses me and starts to turn around, while I increase my pace towards him, reaching into my jacket pocket as I close the gap. He manages to flash a badge and smile before I flash the Saturn 5 out of my pocket and ram it hard into his chest. Right on target—his mouth goes slack and a long breath rattles out. As he staggers back against the wall, the badge dropping from his hand, I look into his eyes, but he doesn't meet my stare, choosing instead to gaze very blankly in the general direction of my bookcase. The rattle stops and he is dead, his legs buckling. I follow him to the floor, hanging onto my Saturn 5, not wanting it to be twisted out of his chest—it's a good plug and I don't want blood on my carpet. I am considering where to stash the body when the phone trills. I sweep it up in one smooth movement.

"Hi, this is Colonel Parker."

I catch sight of myself in the mirror. I look good. I look fucking great.

"Sorry, Colonel, I had a Mr Kempner from the FBI in here just now, talking about that death threat made against you. He wanted to ask you some questions. Has he found you yet?"

Only by violently kicking my left shin with my right heel and biting my left index finger do I manage to stop myself screaming to whoever else is listening that I'm going to stab them repeatedly with a fucking moonrocket until their body is drained of every last drop of blood.

"Um . . . no, I haven't seen Mr . . . ah . . . Kempner . . . did you say *death threat*, Jimbo?" I pick up the remote as I talk, and fire up my wall mounted Bang & Olufsen.

"Yes sir. Some loon who thinks that anyone talking to aliens should be macheted into little pieces. You're the main man, Colonel, so this guy wants to start with you. Guess the Feds have gotta follow it up."

Jimbo's tone implied that the notion of me hacked into little pieces by a mouth-foaming religious fundamentalist was staggeringly funny. Fucking moron. I briefly imagine plucking out Jimbo's eyes with the

Saturn 5 and feeding them to my angel fish, before relenting and making a mental note to have the retard fired instead.

"Yeah, I guess they do. Thanks for the call, Jimbo. No more now, OK? I gotta put my best suit on, gotta date with the alien, remember? I'll speak to Mr Kempner if I see him." Laughing, I cut the connection and turn to the FBI man. He is spread out on his back, a small smile on his face, the Saturn buried to the base of its second stage in his chest. I gently retrieve it. Thankfully, there is hardly any blood on the Saturn and only a slowly spreading stain on his white shirt—not enough to mess my carpet. Good. I drag the body across the office and stuff it in my toy trunk, as 53 Miles West of Venus by the B-52's flows mellifluously from my pen-shaped Bang & Olufsen speakers.

Once, in 1976, the skin of the Viking 2 lander was burnished smooth. Today, it is pitted and scarred, the result of over thirty years bombardment by micrometeorites and abrasive Martian dust. No longer alien in appearance, the lander now looks like a relic of the extinct Martian civilisation that it once came to seek. Bent, battered and long dead, the Viking's parabolic antenna aims beyond the pink sky of Mars and towards a point in the heavens traversed by Earth during its journey around the sun. But the home planet is no longer listening.

Later, suited up and almost ready, I gaze through the west window of the observation deck at the swollen redness of the late afternoon sun. Through the opposite window, I observe my waiting shuttle, less than three kilometres away. I know the shuttle to be a pure white creature, but the setting sun has mutated it into a bloodied vengeful bird of death. A babble of voices floats upward from the waiting phalanx of press, whose defences I must now penetrate to reach the sanctuary of the shuttle. I consider Simpson, with his insane plan to convert the dead beauty of Mars into a festering cesspit of humanity and I am able to put my own madness into a cool perspective. Simpson is dead now, but his kind is too numerous and I cannot stop them on my own. It is my good luck that the Enkassans chose to announce themselves at this critical juncture. Despite their peaceable nature, I'm sure that they have destructive capabilities. All that is required is a little provocation. I drop the Saturn 5 into my flight bag and head for the elevator.

ONE DAY AT A TIME
Hertzan Chimera & M. F. Korn

The two old coots started having the dry heaves as soon as they got WhizBanged out of hyperspace; they were craving alcohol like a gut-shot dog when the scout ship landed. The little verdant plush moon loomed in a pink peach silhouette of a sky from a bustin-out-all-over pregnant mother planet. A gas planet but no sunshine, just a kind of expectant glow that filled the sky with peach like a tequila sunrise.

It was an evanescent beauty when they cocked open the hatch and peered outside, just sniffin' the vegetation and hoping they could find that extra pint of Old Spacehappy Gin that somehow Bill swore he didn't drink, but neither Bill nor Vern knew where this pint of rotgut was. Nonetheless they were having the dt's and the dry heaves. Their ruddy faces were potato spuds of alcohol abuse. They didn't care for the drug supply but popped em back just to keep from dying from cravings.

They saw them arrive, a-coughin' and a-splutterrin'. Damn human folk, they colour shifted indignantly. One of their flock split like ecdysis and fluttered off to Mother Queen to report tonight's attack. They would never win the war these hacking bipeds, never win the war. Back at base, the news was greeted with uproar, "They have sent another attack squad?!?!" went out the chemical horror.

Sea mist of acid acrimony glowed in the sunset on this filthy eating rock 'high in mineral content' as the landlord succinctly put it.

Bill and Vern, eh?

Who'da sent such a troop of nasty dimwits on a conveyancing mission so far into the Death Sector. Did anyone tell them there was no reprieve after their supposed mortality? Did no one brief them about what lay out here? Above and beyond the call of cinnabar or magnetite? Old Bill flicked a juicy cigarillo onto the night sky and unzipped his flies to pee. A boiling mist rose into the FRNEKTA air, his chemical signature would be decoded in days and then you wait and see how friendly the locals would be . . .

The queen hive of the flock was hidden in a hexagonous rhapsody of enclave cliff dwellings and subterraneous mud-dauber holes, each filled with its own small cluster of winged dragon needles, and each of whom had their own library of hallucinogenic wine. Bottled in wax paraffin dart-globule from the thoraxes of winged beauties in the tropical equator of this paradise that was now invaded by enemy morons. The winged ones knew to keep low and spray the area with hallucinogen urine so as to keep the enemy confused.

Vern coughed up some space-phlegm from hyperspace ventilating his arti-lungs cooped up in solid-solid-quiet-quiet until the ship WhizBanged them out into real-time continuum. The upshot of the matter was, that neither Vern nor Bill knew where the hell they were going: they were cannon fodder for any big company mining outfit, or canary in a cage for any big nuclear outfit, that's why they liked to drink, because they knew every time they made their mark back at some outpost for lease-a-space-corpse type outfits they knew they didn't have a Chinaman's chance in hell of coming back half the time, at least with their balls intact and head still sewed on straight.

Vern started to levitate. Bill looked over at him and choked on a bit of phlegm in the back of his rotten old throat. He started tugging at Vern's ankle but there was something like a shine of warm butter in Vern's eyes and Bill could not hold him down. Up Vern drifted, higher and higher into the FRNEKTA atmosphere. From this heady altitude, Vern could see the tactical homebase of the locals, saw their encoded love messages and their blatant torrents of war. He knew they would be an almighty force that could one day take over the network. A rainbow was glowing in the hardwired asshole in the forebrain of Vern McSchulia, he would have his perfect day in Paradise with his Lord to guide him home.

Suddenly, without warning, he fell from the sky—a dot became a splat. Bill ran over as best he could and found Vern on his back in a meteor hole a hundred meters across, laughing his tits off. He had a split lip but that was the extent of his damage. A leaf of torn off rubber sheath flapped about, exposing his false teeth. The guys back at Control couldn't believe Bill had survived such a fall. It was like NASA from the Jimmy Carter Sixties all whoops and high fives.

Bill gave Vern a hand up and Vern smoothed off the outer coating of his split lip so that the wound healed perfectly. The guys at Control readjusted Vern's right eye focus, and night-time rolled in on day one on this haunted planet. The local inhabitants had yet to play their trump card. In the cities, in the hills, a rumbling monster was being uncovered from the moss and the heather. It was not your normal monster, but it had worked every time on any other human intruders they had destroyed. How would 'the monster' work against drunken droids like these two old timers?

Vern crawled back in the ship-pod, and came up smiling android teeth, with a pint of old space happy. That was android electrolyte 'go-juice' that gave them a good buzz-high for hours.

"Where'd you find that, Vern?" Bill asked.

"I ain't a sayin'," Vern said in his redneck-module do-loop voice.

Most of the androids were in a twelve step syntho-alcohol program, as the computerhead scientists found out they were prone to addictions. Some of them got so bad they would just inject the go-juice right into the synthoplastic breastplate.

"You'd better not be holding out on me, Vern!" Bill said with a roar that echoed in the cliffs and canyon underneath the peach sky.

"Why am I seeing you in a vapor trail of speckled dots?"

"You tell me, and why is your face melting like that?"

Because the two droids had runcibles jammed up their buttocks, the boys at Mission Control saw things in real time, although Bill's left eye was cockeyed and out of focus. Light years away, in the control centre, a tech said, "Those morons are goofing on dragonfly urine! I remember this now! We've got to adjust them chemically, bring them down to counteract. Otherwise we aren't going to see anything but android freakyshit for days."

The techguy got onto it and in no time all was well on Planet FRNEKTA. In fact, that was what PrimeTime called their landing on this unchartered territrory, VERN & BILL DRINK TO PLANET

FRNEKTA. It ran to all the major off-world colonies in full syndication. This was their third live season and they had caused quite a storm on any biochemically inhabitable planet they had fallen out of hyperspace near. In the words of the locals of FRNEKTA, "Something had to be done."

And that something came in the form of more gas, I'm afraid. This new gas had been specially formulated to make men (even droid men) burp. Vern and Bill's Primetime burps could be heard all over the interstellar network. Then they sent a gas that made them fart. Then they sent a gas that wired itself into their insult circuits and they were F***ing and Blinding all over the cosmos, live and direct. Then a gas came that made Vern's eyeballs fall out all the time and Bill got a huge erection that made a three foot tent in his stretch fabric daysuit. One by one appalled satellite networks dropped the Vern & Bill live boozathon and soon Control was on the blower asking what the David Copperfield was going on down there. Here's the transcript in cleaned up format:

Control: What the f*** is going, you comedyless jack asses.

Bill: Who the f*** are you? (Bill can be seen looking into the sky dumbly like a Road to Damascus sketch)

Control: We pay your G**damn wages, slipshod, and you address me as Sir!

Vern: Show him your c**k, Bill. Pull the foreskin right back and show him what those commie b******s have done to you with their chemical weapons. Isn't there some sort of space treaty about abuse of the groin? (Vern could be heard farting rather loudly all over the hyperspace intercom)

Bill: I'll show the b******s. (He gets it out and points to an infestation of ants that are growing from the surface of his penis, growing, actually growing in the epidermis and popping out to roam and scurry all over his tickling thighs). This isn't the light entertainment you promised us when we signed the ten series contract. You will be hearing from my shyster!!

Control: We can only recalibrate so far then you guys gotta get drinking. It's that that the customers pay for. They wanna' see ya fall over and have your dirty face hit the s*** or something. Make it slapstick, make it something more than G**damn rude, whydonchya!

Bill: (whispers to Vern) He is hysterical. Let's moon him.

They both show their wrinkled naked hairy baboons assholes and the broadcast is cut.

Never to return to PrimeTime across the cosmos.

But whatever happened to Vern & Bill? Did they move on to better things? Did they get better agents? Better lawyers? Better points gross? Well, let's travel way back through the interstellar mileage and see if the stoopeed pair have gotten off their fat arses just yet . . .

Computer-sweet radio voice announcer-chip:

(Organ Muzak)When we last saw poor Vern and Bill, they had slipped from their sobriety and made utter fools of themselves. During their drunken stupor and hallucinegenic hayride, they climbed down into the queen hive and were suddenly turned into cocoons inside wax paraffin coffins, in a hexadecimal shell of which there was no escape. We here at FRNEKTA decided to put them to sleep for their courage and bravery in the OUTER LIMITS OF NOWHERE SHOW!!!!

(Music crescendos, crash of electronic ink blots, modal frequencies of bifribrial tonality and silent vaporous seas of unity??)

WE WILL BE RIGHT BACK AFTER THIS COMMERCIAL FOR KENDRA EXTREME PLEASURE MODELS.

"My friend, have you ever been stuck in the eight corner pocket of nowhere, somewhere north of Rigel and West of Andromeda? Horny? Foreman up your behonkey? Spend your skin credits on Kendra X, she humps to order and quotes Kipling when she is done! All you gotta do is climb on after you change her skank gasket?"

Switch to:

Asteroid Haemorrhoid Festival on Babylon Tramp Planet !!!!!BRING THE KIDS!!!!!??? . . .

(FADE OUT)

(Organ Music from spherical nodules in every runcible cable station in the known universe?)

APPLAUSE?

(FADE TO WHITE NOISE).

SPIRIT OF RAGE
Iain Darby

As he reached for the door, Care Odell's hand trembled. Surprised, the young priest hesitated, and he looked around, trying to identify the source of his unease. He had never experienced such a feeling before, and it took him a moment to realise what it was. It was with some surprise that he named it. Fear.

He straightened and stepped back, gathering his thoughts. His eyes swept the building before him. The asylum was outside the boundaries of the habitat, the huge dome that covered and protected most of Europe from the ancient anarchy of the skies.

Care had been dropped by an air vessel that had departed in almost indecent haste, as though even the robot pilot had been disturbed by the barren scene.

Four dark towers thrust themselves rudely toward the full moon that filled the sky, their polarised windows reflecting only the barrenness around them.

On all sides of the asylum was empty moorland. Having only ever known the crowded streets of the habitat perhaps it was the emptiness that disturbed him.

He brushed the feeling off. Fear. He chided himself. Fear was a thing of the ancient past. There was no place for it in the modern world.

Purposefully stepping forward, he placed his palm on a door panel, as he had been instructed. A mechanical click signalled the door was unlocking and the door slid to one side. A locked door. A rarity in itself.

As he entered, a white-coated man hurried toward him, a hand outstretched in welcome.

"Father . . . "

"Dr Luther?"

The doctor smiled. "Thank you for coming, Father Odell." He briefly grasped Care's hand.

Care smiled in return, his self-assurance returning as he basked in the doctor's obvious pleasure at his arrival.

"We all serve at the habitat's pleasure."

"Indeed," agreed the doctor. "If you'd be so good as to follow me . . . "

He led Care through a labyrinthine complex of corridors whose walls traced the age of this ancient building, their coverings dirty and torn, a thin network of cracks stretching from floor to ceiling. Care, so used to the geometric perfection of the habitats, shuddered in dismay.

At last Dr Luther led him into a more carefully maintained lounge area. Couches pressed themselves against the wall, and a tea machine bubbled a welcome. Dr Luther bade him sit while he prepared their beverages.

"Until yesterday I had no idea that such places as this existed," Care told him. "Asylum. A place of refuge or shelter." He smiled self-consciously. "I looked it up."

Dr Luther passed him a piping hot lemon tea and sat across from him. "There is another, less archaic, definition," he said quietly, sipping at his tea. "An institution for the mentally unbalanced. That is a more correct definition in this case, Father. Few know that such places exist. It would trouble the people of the habitats, and why disturb their tranquillity?"

"Yet there must always be some like yourself, willing to shelter and care for the poor, unbalanced minds amongst us," added Care.

"Indeed," agreed the Doctor. "So a few *are* informed. Those who are, are chosen carefully."

"And now I am to join you in the care of these unfortunates." Yesterday, Care had been summoned to the Bishop's office to be told of his new mission.

It had only been the second time in his life he had been in that grand place, its silk hung walls adorned by reproductions of ancient masterpieces. Two candles burned atop a small altar pressed against one wall. Between them, exquisite in its detail, was a tiny golden statue of the Christ figure, smiling and fat, prayer beads in each of his six hands.

The Bishop was a small figure behind his great oaken desk. He had not stood to greet Care, and Care had hurried to the side of the desk and knelt before him, his head low.

The Bishop fondly stroked the back of Care's head. The old man's voice seemed regretful. "We will be sorry to lose you, my boy, even for a little while."

Care looked up. The Bishop's eyes had been heavy with the love of the habitat. "Your teachings have been quite inspirational."

The memory of his words warmed Care. Like all members of the habitats, he was secure in the knowledge that his fellows valued his worth, just as he valued theirs.

He brought himself back to the present. Dr Luther was still talking, shaking his head.

"No, Father. We didn't ask for a priest to help care for our patients. We are well able to deal with disturbed individuals here, Father. With time and careful treatment we can help them. In time all who come here are cured, all except one. There is one we cannot help." Luther's voice struck a bitter note. "His sickness isn't of the mind or the body. His sickness resides in the seat of his soul."

"One man? I have been transferred from the Seminary to care for one man?"

Luther set down his tea, the cup rattling slightly in its saucer. "If man he is. I saw you hesitate, outside the door, on our security cameras . . ."

"Yes," agreed Care. "I had a peculiar feeling. A feeling of dread."

"It radiates out from him, Father. Dread, terror . . . rage."

Care's eyebrows drew together. Rage and terror were not words heard in the habitat, least of all in the mouths of educated men like the doctor.

Seeing his confusion, the doctor hurriedly waved one hand in apology. "Forgive me, Father, I speak of things you do not know. And I have strayed from the point. No. In answer to your question, you are not required to care for this man. You have been requested to care for the staff."

"The staff?"

"Working with Kintana, I'm sorry, that is his name—Kintana—working with Kintana has a negative impact. One of my colleagues thinks it is a virus. Perhaps it is. A virus of the mind. Some of the attendants, staff members have been acting strangely. There have been incidents," he hesitated. "Assaults."

"Assaults? Physical violence? On one habitat member against another?"

"Yes."

"What has been done?"

"They remain here, but not as staff," said Luther sadly.

Inwardly, Care recited a mantra of reassurance. *Order in all, peace in order, contentment in peace, peace in the habitat, order in all.* One of the first he had learned at the seminary. He felt his perplexity fade in the familiarity of the words. "What is required of me?" he asked.

"As we care for him, you care for us. Help us maintain the balance of the habitat, even here, outside its domain."

There was such pain in his voice that Care felt a surge of compassion greater than any had known heretofore.

"Of course, I will, my son," he told him, patting Luther's head as the doctor fell to his knees before him. "Of course I will."

Each day they would come to him, nurses, doctors, attendants, Luther himself. They would come, and hesitantly at first, then in the relief of their unburdening, in a torrent of words, they would confess the sins that plagued them.

Their words varied. Some spoke of feelings of irritation, annoyance. Others of impulses building to a crescendo that cried out to be resolved through angry words and bitter recriminations. A few, those who had most contact with Kintana, spoke of worse. They spoke of dreams that came unbidden, dreams of torment and torture.

Care let them empty their negativity into him, drained each drop of it, replacing it with hope and order, speaking softly of the perfection of the habitat. The safety of blessed routine and contentment. Where they had come from, where they would soon return to.

He would pray with them, sharing the most soothing of mantras.

He taught them techniques that would allow them to house such feelings in a small corner of their mind. That would let them lock the door of that house and pass the key to him.

Day by day they came, and day by day it became harder.
Until . . .
"I would like to see him."
"I don't think that would be wise, Father," said Doctor Luther.
"I have helped all the others. I have helped you. Perhaps I could help him."

Care could tell by Luther's expression that he did not think that likely, but Luther's confessions to him had changed their relationship and there was no possibility of Luther forbidding him.

"Please, arrange it," ordered Care.

"Ah, the Priest they talk so much of. I wondered when you would come, Priest."

Care blinked, Kintana was so unlike what he had expected. He was old. His hair, though shorn to the scalp, was snow white. Dark rings circled his eyes. He sat on a bunk, his hands manacled, a long iron chain bolted to the floor allowing him only a few feet's movement from the bed.

Stick thin, he stood, moving toward Care until he reached the limit of the chains. Care could see the quiet tension in those muscles as they strained against the chain. Care was still out of reach.

Suddenly Kintana relaxed. His tone was mocking. "Don't worry, Priest. I won't harm you. Perhaps I'll help you."

"Help me? How?"

"Perhaps I can show you another way, a better way."

"That is what I have come to show you." Very slowly, Care moved closer.

Kintana eyes remained fixed on him. "Ah, your hotchpotch of religion. All bits of this and bits of that."

"The best of all the old beliefs brought together in one. Recognising that each sought the same thing."

Kintana grinned a cat's grin, amused and dangerous. "Order," he breathed.

"Order," agreed Care, calmly, "for in order there is peace. Let me share a little of it with you."

"By all means." Kintana sat down on the bed, and with an exaggerated gesture invited Care to join him.

Carefully, Care sat, taking a moment to glance into the corner of the cell where a blinking red light assured him that Luther and an attendant were watching, would come to his aid in an instant.

"Let us begin with a prayer," he said. "Habitat, home, safe under dome, content in . . . "

"Habitat home, a plastic dome, built to keep out radiations that have not been a danger, in ten generations . . . " Kintana aped him.

Care ignored his blasphemy. "Content in our place," he continued. "Loving each other . . . "

"You believe in reincarnation?" asked Kintana sharply. "That you have lived before, that we have all lived before?"

Care paused. "Yes," he said. "Each incarnation was a learning experience, and through the lives we have lived to this point, we have accumulated a mass of experience that has made us what we are today. Productive members of the habitat."

"Except me."

"You will be," Care assured him. Quietly, he finished the prayer. Toward the end, closing his eyes and without any hint of mockery, Kintana joined in.

At its end he opened them. "Thank you."

Care stood. "I will return tomorrow," he told him, pleased. The man simply needed to be shown some compassion, as all men did. Kintana seemed less dangerous now, just a sad old man, cruelly chained. He lowered his head and Care placed a hand on his scalp in blessing, and suddenly . . .

He sat before the mouth of a cave, behind him the mournful wailing of the woman he had stolen filled his ears, but he ignored the noise. He belched loudly, the noise proudly announcing his full stomach.

An old man neared, and he lifted his club and growled. When the old one screamed a reply he swung his club, shattering the old man's skull with one blow.

Figures appeared on the ground before him. Men, their appearance as wild as his, shaggy-manned and fur clad. Some waved long sticks, others clubs. They stood a short way from his cave, yelling and screaming. Like the woman, they were tall. Tall, but thin and weak.

He stood, his belly full of meat, and lifted his bloodied club. He had enjoyed the woman, if they had others they too would be his. Swinging the club above his head he ran at the nearest of them.

He gasped, drawing his hand from Kintana's scalp as though it had burned him. Kintana tilted his head to face him. He was smiling again. A feral, knowing smile.

"Troubled, Father?"

Care stepped back from him. Banging on the door for the attendant to give him exit. He paused in the open doorway, looking back at Kintana. Very slowly, very deliberately he told him, "I will return tomorrow."

Outside he drew deep panting breaths. Hurrying to his own room he knelt by his bed and struggled to find a calming mantra. The vision had been so real. He had felt the meat in his stomach, seen the woman struggling beneath his bulk.

That Kintana had somehow engineered it, through hypnosis or some subtle form of autosuggestion, Care had no doubt, but it felt none-the-less real for that knowledge.

The next day Care was more cautious and stayed out of Kintana's reach. "What did you do yesterday?" he asked him.

"Do?"

"You made me imagine something. Something primitive. Something . . . violent."

Kintana simply grinned at him.

"You are sick, my son," whispered Care.

Kintana's eyes narrowed, and Care felt a thrill of fear, like a small electric shock, pass through his body.

"It is you that are sick," Kintana said, "in your sterile world, your empty passionless palaces."

"You are young, Father. Can you not feel the hot blood coursing through your veins?"

"I know what you speak of, but the sexual impulse led to conflict—there cannot be harmony where there is conflict. It was bred out of us long ago."

"Bred out! Bred out!" roared Kintana. "And what is the result? Sexless, soulless people, who know nothing of excitement, of the passion and fury of life. People that merely walk and breathe, and mouth meaningless platitudes from the day they are born 'til the day they die."

He shook his head. "In the clean world that you have made—where did you think that passion, that rage has gone? Study your history—it was there. Did you think it ceased to exist? Study your physics. Matter cannot be altered."

"Rage is not a thing of atoms and electrons," pointed out Care.

"Is it not, Father? Are you sure? Is evil not a thing you can feel in the very air about you? Fear not a cloak that wraps itself around you?" He strained against his bonds, and Care retreated even further from him, speaking as he did so.

"Why then has it gathered itself in you?"

Kintana eyes became wild as he shouted his reply, shaking his chains, showering Care with spittle. "Because I am an appropriate vessel. One that will spill over, out into the world." Suddenly he stopped struggling against his restraints and grinned. "Perhaps I'll spill a little rage into you."

"There is no room for rage in me," answered Care, gently.

"You have family, father?" Kintana's voice was even, cunning, and Care felt the hairs begin to rise on the back of his neck.

"My mother is still alive."

"And if I went to the Munich quarter and slit the throat of your mother, how would that make you feel?"

"It would sadden me . . . " Care stopped. "Who told you my mother lives in Munich?"

"It would do more than sadden you priest. Would it not enrage you? Fill you with a desire for revenge? And if not, then did you truly love her at all?"

Care took a step forward and Kintana laughed. "Rage lives, priest, it just has to find the right vessel."

After that the dreams came every night.

The smoke in the trench was thick, its acrid odour catching at his throat, burning the sensitive lining, stinging his eyes. He blinked hard, tears trying to give him some relief. Shells spilled down from the skies with the sharp crack of a thousand thunders. A wet trickle of urine ran down his leg, and he gripped his rifle tighter . . .

Doctor Luther was concerned for him and worry lines wrinkled his brow. "You haven't seen any members of staff since you met him," he said.

"I need a little time for contemplation," lied Care. "A day or two, that's all."

He waited in the dark of an alley, listening to the woman's approach, stiletto heels clicking a quick time march across the cobbled pavement. The knife was slick in his sweating palm, the need in his groin urgent.

A week passed, Luther visiting him every day, becoming ever more vexed.

"You aren't eating. You look . . . " He struggled to find the appropriate words, but Care knew from the look on his face what his appearance must be like.

"Another day . . . "

He held a dying child in his arms, a hundred children, a thousand, and they were all his. Lovers spurned him, loved him, left him, died.

On a street in Calcutta street thugs laughed, bully's laughter, unkind, excited. Expectant. They expected him to weep, to beg for mercy. He would do none of those things. All he felt was the overwhelming weight of inevitability.

He knew what they would do, for he had done it a thousand times before. Beat and been beaten.

He screamed.

The attendant trembled before Care, as he opened the door of Kintana's cell.

Dawn had not yet broken, and Kintana had been sleeping. He rose from his bed, rubbing the sleep from his eyes.

"Stop it," demanded Care.

"Stop what?" inquired Kintana innocently.

"Your lives. The reason for your rage. Stop showing me your lives."

Kintana laughed and Care was chilled by the real pleasure he heard in the sound.

"They aren't my lives," he said. "They're yours. Surely you know yourself?"

Aghast, Care stared at him for a moment, then he turned, banging on the door to be let out.

Tears filling his eyes, he ran, stumbling past the attendant. Kintana's laughter pursued him down the corridor.

Doctor Luther came to see him an hour later. "The patient has died," he told him.

Care looked up at him, surprised. "Died?"

"A cancer. I've known for a while," explained Luther.

Care thoughts raced. No one had mentioned a cancer. A cancer that kills in an hour? He opened his mouth to ask a question, but Luther placed a hand on his elbow.

"I watched, " he said. "On the monitor."

"He cannot hurt you any more. He cannot hurt anyone any more."

Care let his questions die in his mouth.

"I have contacted the seminary. Told them your work here is completed. The Bishop is waiting to welcome you back."

Care nodded dumbly. They did not speak again.

In the time before the airship arrived to take him home, Care collected his few things. Bathed and shaved, pressed the perfect uniform that he wore.

The ship took him directly to the seminary, depositing him in its beautiful gardens. He was met there and escorted to the Bishop's office once more.

Left alone to wait for the great man, he admired again the little statue. He lifted it, surprised at its lack of weight. It was hollow, and when he examined it closely he could see that the gold colour was peeling in places, revealing grey metal beneath.

Replacing it on the altar, he lifted each of the silk hangings. Behind one he found what he was seeking. He pulled at it, a panelled section of thin wall, revealing the air conditioning duct behind. He broke off a length of the ducting tube. The hard metallic weight of the pipe was satisfying in his hand. It had no edge, but wielded properly its weight would serve.

He settled down to wait for the Bishop.

OCTOBER EYES
Alison L. R. Davies

Devil's guts—a sprawling maze of fern-like viscera that clings to my bare feet as I wander the lawn. Yes, I told him long ago to get rid of it, to scrape away those shards of greenery, but he merely skimmed the surface, iron fork raised in anger at the world. Always fighting the voices inside, he failed to hear my whispered assurances, "If you don't get the roots, if you don't clip every shoot, it will come back, and more menacing than the last time."

Now it infiltrates my nakedness with raw fingers, and somehow, the imagined sensations that tickle my feet make me smile. It was always his problem. He never loved the mysteries of the garden like I did. There's something soulless about a man who fails to communicate with nature. I pause at the brink of the turf, sniffing the warm, oily milk of the soil. Further up the path a bird sits, chest puffed in contemplation, eyes watching me. I can see it is curious, afraid but inquisitive as to my next move. But I have no ulterior motive. I knew he would return, even before he left. Ours is a love that cannot be questioned. We show it in different ways, no feather-soft cooing and lips upon skin, or hands slick with the dampness of need, of belonging. We don't do that, for it would be for show. Instead, our love circles the ether like ripples of air, stretching and pulling us backwards. I know what he is thinking, and he knows my heart. I try not to turn, but I feel displacement of air, the faint vibrations of movement from the house. He is back. His key clicking in certainty, forcing gusts of October wind through the hall. He stands there for a moment, just like he always does. Face determined, grimacing as the dust mites swim up his nostrils and prod at his chin. He can see them spiralling the staircase, and I know what he is thinking, "Lazy cow, can't be bothered to dust, too much like hard work." He moves then, cautiously through the hall. Knowing that I won't be there, that the garden has always been more of a home to me than these four walls. But even so, he pretends. It's a ritual we have perfected for some time. I think I hear my name. "Karen, oh Karen," soft, a forced murmur that chokes back a million emotions. And my bird-like friend hears it too, up, up he flies, taking a flurry of leaves with him.

He moves inside the Kitchen now. The scrape of aluminium, of Formica surfaces and the clutter of cutlery sings through the house. It takes me back, leads my wisp-like fingers to the moment he left. The day I can never forget. His anger was a like a separate entity, smarting the air with a dialogue so foul that my eyes bled at its fervour. There are some things beyond comprehension, some schools of thought that will always be misunderstood. And that was his problem. He couldn't see beyond the filth and the mud, beneath the crawling earth that swallowed his footsteps. He looked at me like I was nothing, like my ideas, the very essence of my imaginings could be squashed in seconds like an insect. My body faltered; a papery moth crumbled to dust by his rage. And then he left. Cleaning and scavenging through the house, packing his things in carrier bags with knots and holes and ugly wet fingerprints. But I knew even then—he would be back.

And the garden was my only refuge in the long days of Summer: I trampled through the wildflowers, pale, burning skin against an unforgiving sun. I learnt the secrets of the grasses that warmed my soul, drank from their wisdom and waited (the patient wife that I am) for the return of my errant love. I took to the ways of the wild, listening to the gossip of the silver birch, humming an early morning wake up call with the birds. These things became my comfort, my lover's kiss. But still I longed for the real thing, the feel of his merciless lips pressing their urgency into my mind.

"Karen, I'm so sorry." He's calling now; words heavy like the bruise-swollen clouds, like my October eyes. I can feel him tormented, muscles aching, mouth parched, he longs for another chance, a fresh start in the Autumn of our romance. But Winter has set in with a cruel certainty, teasing the delicate shafts where baby shoots lay, flaying the mossy flesh of the land with its icy nails. And I know there is only a sliver of chance that we can start again. He yanks at the patio doors, heaving panes of glass aside to step into the cold. I wait for him to come over, I know that he will. He moves, no longer the self-assured, the demon possessed, no . . . this time he sways like a toddler, stumbling with vulnerability. He's scouring the grass, searching for something that cannot be found. Part of me wants to cry out, to smooth that ruddy skin with my brittle hands, to feel him above me once more, as he moves with passion and fury. But my voice fails me, and then the ground is upon me, quietening my soul, sucking my vengeful spirit back into its earthy grave.

"You had to do it, didn't you," he's saying now, moaning through bush and bark and thick dampness. "You had to push me too far. And I never meant to, Karen, I really didn't, but you know how the anger takes over. I've tried to control it, but it's like the devil, it's way too powerful a thing."

I shiver. Am I supposed to feel sorry for him now? But it's okay, the garden won't let me, it puts protective arms around me, and I know he can't hurt me again. He's crying now, leaning so close that I can almost smell the sourness of his spittle, of raw eggs and yesterday's cheap liquor. He moves a hand on the soil, stroking, pawing, but the earth keeps a tight grip on me. His hands become dirty, visibly dirty, as opposed to the other well kept sins that lie beneath the grain. He shoves at the earth, kneading and pulling, moving the hastily discarded rake to one side. And when he is done, pity concealed in the mud, he rocks back on his heels stretching his face to the sky. Moaning a silent prayer for release and I know that this is his last visit. He turns then, quick and sharp, scratching shoe-leather against stone, he curses the ground as his laces cling to the gummy vines of the Devil's guts. It snags, pulling his foot from under him, the sprawling tendrils have him firmly within their grasp, and he falls, face to the soil. The iron prongs of the rake tear their meat gently, consumed into the pinkness of his belly by sheer body weight. I feel him struggling above me, not in the throes of passion, but in another such sweet agony. And this time it is for my great joy, for my pleasure. Softly now, the intestinal wall gives itself up in a tidal wave, watering the earth with rich fatty tissue and warm blood. I sigh, my deathbed finally complete by his

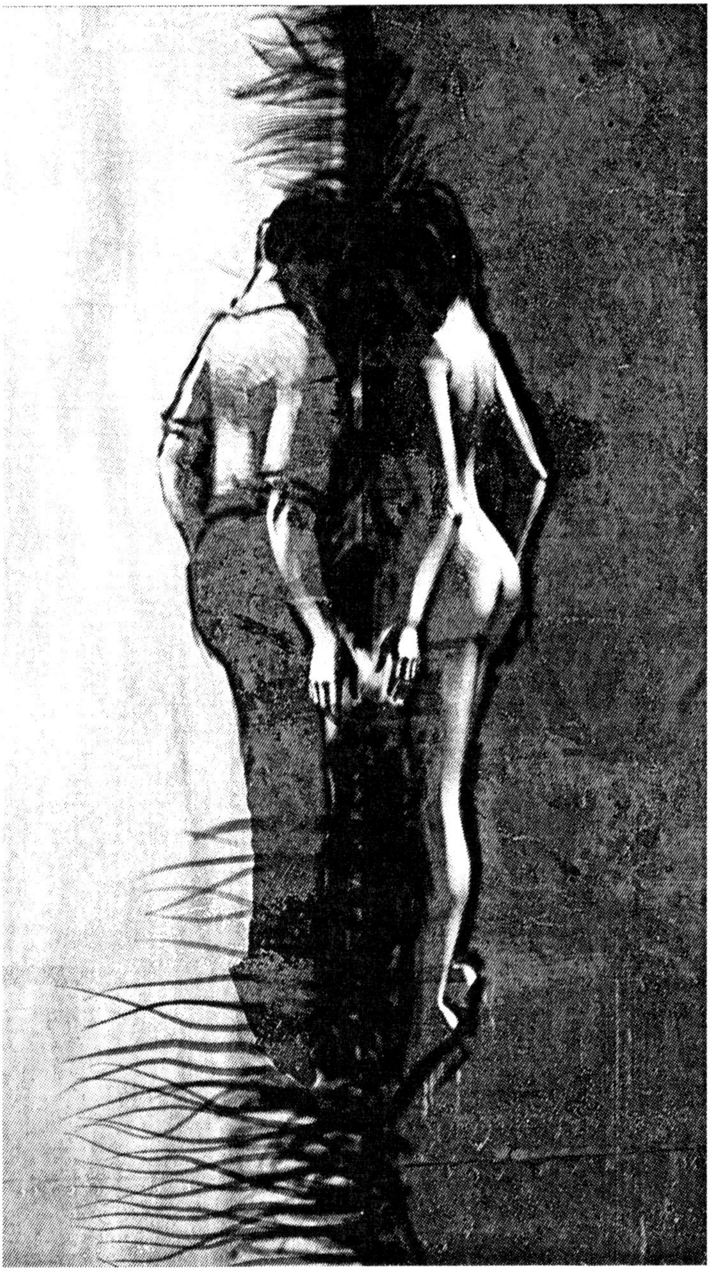

presence. The garden is abundant, gloriously awash with colour, just as I always wished, leaving the Devil's Guts free to roam and pillage like the scavenger perennial it is.

MR OCTOBER
Jack Fisher

Mr October has tasted peach blossoms and pumpkin juice before. He's propped himself up against the back of summer winds and unexpected rainstorms and has waited for autumn in cold, open fields to pipe night clouds and dust from his silvery mouth. Mr October walks down the streets that are strewn with confetti and rainbow-coloured leaves and dips his candlestick fingers into the eye sockets of freshly cut pumpkins.

Children run through ghosts that have uprooted themselves from leaf-beds and hide in between the sidewalk cracks. They have pillowcases full of candy that bounce and swing at their sides. Dozens of doors open to them and behind each stands someone with bowls of rot. They run and kick their feet with the night in their hair. Others hang from oak boughs with Chiclet fangs, and their arms crossed over their chests. They swing back and forth like bats until they're tagged and then they're off again robbing the night of sweets.

Mr October skips across the street as the champagne-coloured dusk turns to plum-coloured dark behind him. The smell of cinnamon and herbs swim the winds. He passes a dilapidated mailbox atop which sits a mangy black cat. It hisses and claws at the wind (cats can see ghosts). Mr October scans the town with firefly eyes and smiles. He walks carefully; if he were to fall, he'd bleed magnificent, fluorescent colours of orange and he wouldn't mend until next October. The children run through him, passing silvery shadows through his frame. They take in his scent: cold night air, leaves, candy, make-up, pumpkins, and thrill.

He walks with a smile as he comes to the end of the town. His face is the colour of ash and orange commingled. There are shadows under his eyes from Time now. He opens his overcoat to reveal a landscape of far-off galaxies. Flaming meteorites and comets race by, crossing through the Milky Way and across the faces of stars. Mr October stands still in the middle of the moon-coloured road in a swirl of night-time dust at the border of a new town, a new Land, a new Time.

Behind him, children continue to hoot and carry on. Goblins and beasts run past him and not once do they see him. Mr October is that of the elements, he is of October, of Halloween. The shapes on his abdomen hiss and buzz until his entire torso is raining crisp Oak and Maple leaves. Behind them, the faces of pumpkins flicker out and steam. The children are there, too! They're seen running dressed like the dead, then as ghosts, and then they fall into shadowy ghost realms. The trees growl, leaves kick up into mini tornadoes, and the shutters on the houses flap like coffin lids.

October has passed through the town as silent as a ghost. The spirits die, the smells, the crisp, crystalline winds die down for the season. Masks come off, skins are stripped, and bags of sweets are emptied to rot. The children build tree forts in the open arms of an old Oak or Willow tree and wait with cold, cracked lemon-sunshine in their hair and mouths.

"Where has it gone?" they exclaim. "It's passed by so fast!"

Mr October closes his overcoat and it's all over. Halloween walked its way through the small towns of the world, every last one of them, with the empty, ever-faithful carcasses of Time in his path. A robust, chilly breeze kicks up, nice and heavy, and Mr October is gone, in a whirlwind of twisted Maple leaves, with the snap of one of his candlestick fingers.

PAY PER VIEW
Jess Butcher

"JESUS, YOU MORON!" he screeched. "WHAT YOU TRYIN' TO DO, CUT M'DAMN EAR OFF?"

Jack 'Spider' O'Malley was seated in a musty recliner in front of the living room window, a soiled bath towel draped over his shoulders as the barber went about her work.

"Hay rakes and hail stones, woman," he muttered, "I'm gonna end up lookin' like a damn Doberman if you don't quit snippin' my ears every time I need a trim."

The barber exhaled noisily through her nostrils and stepped back, hands on ample hips. The room was awash in the late evening glow seeping through an ancient, curled window shade. She eyed him malevolently for a moment, thinking the hateful old man looked even more demonic than usual in the dirty, dying light.

"You want me to finish this or not?" she asked contemptuously.

Lillian 'Muffin' Christmas had been cutting Jack O'Malley's hair for over twenty years now. Like her mother before her, she tended to O'Malley's tonsorial needs every Saturday night as he perched in front of the television observing his life-long passion, professional wrestling.

Muffin's flat, pig-eyes blazed, liquid splotches blurred behind thick lenses. Her head tilted to one side, a single hairpin holding her wig precariously in place, a matted, crimson arthropod clinging desperately to life atop a desert outcrop.

"It would help if you'd let me turn on a lamp," she said. "I can't see a darn thing."

"You fat, helpless pig. You couldn't see nothin' if you was sittin' in the park at high noon on the Fourth of July!" he snorted laughter, lifting his hands to his face, thumbs and index fingers curled to cruelly mimic Muffin's thick eyeglasses.

Muffin had grown accustomed to this taunting jackal over the course of the past forty years. She'd hated him since the first moment she laid eyes on him.

•

"My sweet Muffin." Her mother had smiled as she bent to kiss the chubby six year-old. "Please say 'hello' to Mr O'Malley, honey. He's going to stay for dinner."

"Yeah, hi kid," the scarred man with one hideous, yellow eye snarled. "Here's a present for you, yer momma said you liked presents."

The stranger shoved a brown paper sack at the little girl as she hid behind her mother. "Here kid, take it. What's wrong with you, you stupid or somethin'?"

Muffin's mother brought home a lot of men, but none frightened and repulsed the little girl quite as much as this one.

"He's just kidding you, Muffin. Here, look what we've brought you," she said, taking the sack from O'Malley and removing the gift.

"Mrs Potato Head!" the plump first-grader beamed.

"What do you say, honey?" her mother coaxed her.

"Thank you, Momma, thank you Mr . . . "

"You can call me Spider," he snarled. "Looks like yer shaped about like 'ol Mrs Spud Head there yourself," he smiled evilly, a portent of things to come.

Jack O'Malley was no father figure. By 1957, the stocky, violent man had spent ten years traveling the highways and back roads of Florida and Georgia, wrestling in carnivals as 'Spider' O'Malley. Sidelined and drifting as the result of an injury, O'Malley met Muffin's mother as he sipped beer in the barbecue joint where she worked as a waitress.

Spider told the widowed and gullible Mrs Christmas that he'd recently lost an eye while wrestling 'Kisser' Bill Pfaff at the Tupelo County Fair. The story explained his eye and simultaneously impressed the hefty waitress with his physical prowess.

In truth, O'Malley had lost his eye in a post-contest brawl with Kisser Bill in Tupelo. The two had been embroiled in a smoldering disagreement over the affections of Kisser Bill's traveling companion, *Cleopatra, Exotic Princess of the Nile*, the carnival's headline hootchi-cootchi dancer. Their disagreement peaked on the carnival midway where Kisser Bill threw O'Malley through the front of a hot dog stand and then smashed a gallon jar of catsup over the drunken Irishman's head.

After dinner, O'Malley approached the little girl as she played with her new toy. As dishes clattered in the background, he stood for a long moment, silently appraising Muffin. She was busy, tongue pushed to one side of parted lips as she constructed Mrs Potato Head's face on the white oval of Styrofoam plastic which had come inside the toy box.

"You damn little moron," he taunted her. "Yer s'posed to stick them pieces on a tater, not on that damn piece of foam."

"Can't waste a potato," she said, never looking up at him.

He reached down and crushed the plastic between his meaty fingers. "Yer s'posed to stick 'em on a tater," he said coldly.

Even had O'Malley told Mrs Christmas the truth about his injury, the widow would likely have asked him to stay on. Rural Georgia held little opportunity for a stout, middle-aged woman with a young child. Ignorance and loneliness drove her to Spider, guile and evil desperation inspired him to stay . . . for a lifetime.

•

After forty years, Muffin Christmas stands, gazing at the shrunken, muttering shell of the man she has grown to accept as the embodiment of all things evil.

"C'mon, pig, just finish cuttin' my damn hair, and keep your trap shut. My Pay per View is fixin' to start."

•

Ten minutes later, Muffin removes the scissors from the gaping wound in Spider's throat. His gurgling has diminished to a faint clucking now as she walks to her bedroom and brings back the white plastic fixture her wig rests on each night. Placing the Styrofoam head on the magazine covered TV stand next to his chair, she pinches Spider's fleshy earlobe between her thumb and forefinger.

"You're supposed to stick the pieces on a tater," she whispers as she begins her work.

ROBIN HOOD'S NEW MOTHER
Rhys Hughes

Nina, the Queen of the Amazons, wants to go somewhere different this year. She is bored with Lake Karatis, despite its giant snakes. She has wrestled most of them anyway. She uncorks her little god and whispers into the jar: "Any suggestions for a holiday?"

The shape inside heaves like a bosom. "The Forest of Sherwood."

"Where in all Scythia is that?"

"Beyond its western horizon. Cross the Caucasus and follow the Black Sea coast with the Pontine Mountains on your left. Turn sharp right at Byzantium. I don't know the way from there. You'll have to ask. Perhaps the Emperor can help you."

She frowns and rattles the jar. "Not in Scythia, you say? Well that's original. But what's so special about this Sherwood Forest?"

"It's the home of an outlaw."

"But I'm always catching those and poking them with spears!"

The shape within seems to chuckle. "This one is different. He is the Prince of Thieves. He steals from the rich and gives to the poor. You are very rich and so he will try his luck with you. He is fearless and has the luck of a legend. A good match."

"You are right, little god! It has to be better sport than monstrous serpents. I shall pack my things at once. But how do you get to learn of such strange people and events? After all, you're stuck in there all day."

"I dream about them, mistress. I was the Khazar god of dreaming before you captured me. Now my people never dream. And they are too tired to sleep."

Nina replaces the cork. She is almost excited.

•

The Sheriff of Nottingham is a villain, but he just follows orders, so it isn't his fault. Following orders is much harder than following a road. You have to leap from one instruction to the next, never knowing where they are taking you, like stepping stones over a river of scorpions, either marching packed tight down a dry channel, or else floating on broad leaves, depending on the season, but a difficult feature to cross all the same, and always a suspicion that the next stone will tip up and throw you greaves over helm into the torrent of sting. And the poison forming little tributaries.

"Guy of Gisborne! Come in here at once!"

"Yes, your Sheriffness?"

"Can you guess what I'm doing now? Three Guesses!"

"Um, being a villain?"

"Damn it! How do you keep winning this game? Take a draught of mead as your reward. Now then, I have a problem. I can't follow these orders."

"King John asked you to dress in lingerie again?"

"Would to heaven he had! No, Guy, this is far more awkward than that. See this letter I'm holding? No, not in that hand, which is under the table. This hand! That's right, in front of your face. I know these Norman helmets make you cross-eyed with their nose-guards. Anyway, it was delivered a few minutes ago, don't ask how, all right, carrier pigeon if you must know, and it has come all the way from the Emperor of Byzantium, Isaac II Angelos."

"Oh, him. We don't owe him any allegiance, do we?"

"I wish we didn't, because he has asked me to expect an honoured guest, the Queen of the Amazons. I'm supposed to put her up here in my castle and introduce her to the outlaw Robin Hood. She wants to challenge him to a fight."

"That will save us the trouble, won't it?"

"No, no, no! Don't you remember? You mortally wounded him yesterday!"

•

Robin Hood is dying in a comfortable bed with Maid Marian and Little John in the same room. They made the bed. Little John always has difficulties with duvet covers, he's so clumsy. Robin can feel lumps in the bedding pressing down on his wounds. It's not so merry. He is delirious and mutters strange phrases.

"Go take a Frying Tuck at the moon!"

"What's that he's saying?" asks Little John.

Maid Marian shrugs. "Probably connected with forest business. That's all he ever thinks about. Greenwood this, greenwood that. Bash a holy man on the head, rummage his surplice for his surplus. Code of honour, squirrels."

"Red or grey?"

"I don't believe the latter have been introduced yet."

"No I meant the holy men. Cardinal or monk."

"Ah, bishops mostly. But you know that surely? You did it!"

"I was trying to make small-talk."

They twiddle each other's thumbs, but it's just friendly, not romantic. Then they sigh and scratch their chins and shrug.

"This is taking ages. Perhaps we ought to ease his pain with some poison?"

"Sorry, the river's clean out of scorpions."

"You could hit him with your quarterstaff for a bit."

"I left it in the little room under the stairs at Will Scarlet's house."

"You are simple, John, sometimes!"

Before he can agree, Robin Hood suddenly sits up. His delirium has cleared just for an instant. He has to act quick before it returns.

"Fetch me my bow! I shall fire an arrow out of this window. Where it lands, you must bury me under there!"

He fires the arrow. He falls back. The recoil has finished him off.

•

The Khazar god of dreaming is yawning through his glass walls. It has been a long journey from Scythia, through Turkey and Greece and

Illyria and the Holy Roman Empire and France, and across the Channel to England. Now they are on the edge of Sherwood Forest and it is time to stop yawning, not because things have got interesting, but due to the lack of oxygen inside the sealed jar. There is none left to inhale. He feels sleepy, drunk on his own odour.

"Hi in there! We're here at last!"

The cork pops and he gazes up at the lips of his mistress. They are red and swollen like his eyelids, but bigger and more kissable, depending on who you are, or who you aren't. One day he will jump up and grab for her tongue and refuse to release it until she guarantees his freedom, but if he did that she wouldn't be able to shout the command to let him go, and a stalemate would ensue. And she has more stamina than him.

"Do you require my advice on something?"

"Yes. Where must I walk to find this Robin Hood?"

"Take one step into the forest and he will come to you."

"Did you dream that or make it up?"

"Fiction is not my strength, alas!"

"Good. So we'll fight the duel and then go back to that nice Sheriff of Nottingham's castle for a cup of tea. What do you think?"

"Hush! I hear a sound. A whoooooshing noise!"

"O bloody bugger, I've been shot!"

So she has. The arrow protrudes from her lower abdomen. She doesn't stagger, but merely leans on a tree for support. Scythia suddenly seems as far away as it really is.

•

Guy of Gisborne is riding across the meadows. His surcoat flaps behind him. His chain-mail sparkles in the sun, spoiled in places by grass stains. Perhaps he has recently *greengowned* a maid, as the polite expression has it for outdoor fucking, before he felt compelled, or was ordered, to ride somewhere, don't know where, he probably doesn't either, though it's not a routine mission, nor is he a routine cross-eyed bully, but blond and square jawed and a little bit effete but tough too, in calf and arm. Where are you going, Guy? That's what the leaves seem to whisper in the wind as he enters the forest. But his helm fits so tightly over his ears that he doesn't hear.

The hooves of his horse kick up little twigs and clods of earth. This is no official route through the greenwood. So he knows he is heading the right way. The outlaws tend to move stealthily, like gibbons, whatever those are, through the trees, leaving no print or clue on the ground below. He still has no firm destination in mind. It's just a question of trusting his intuition and avoiding the obvious paths. When he least expects it, he will come across what he seeks. But as he continues to ride through thicker undergrowth and nettles slap his mount's flanks for free, though some men of his acquaintance in York would pay good money for that, or else in kind, which is unkind, the first real doubts enter his brain.

Therefore he comes across a small gathering. He has traversed nearly the whole forest, almost coming out the other side.

He sees Nina, Queen of the Amazons, idling against a tree.

"Your Queeness!" he cries. "I have been sent by my master, the Sheriff of Nottingham, to confess that Robin Hood is probably already dead. Sorry. He couldn't bear to tell you when you were in his castle. But his conscience bothered him."

"Does he have one?" she mutters.

"Well he is a villain, but it isn't his fault, so yes!"

He looks around at the assembled company. He draws his sword with a cry.

"Hello," say Maid Marian and Little John.

"Ooh, you blighters! What are you doing here?"

"We've come to bury Robin."

"Can't you do that in your own time? I'm busy!"

"We have to bury him where the arrow landed."

They point and Guy of Gisborne follows the line of their converging fingers.

"What? Inside Nina, the Queen of the Amazons?"

"That was his final request. Code of chivalry and all that. Awkward, that's for sure. No help for it. We're just following orders. And stuff."

•

Nina, Queen of the Amazons, feels in a quandary. She is lying down in the middle of a clearing. She is very cold. Maid Marian, Little John and Guy of Gisborne have gone to fetch the body of the outlaw Robin Hood. They have also gone to collect a sharp knife, a needle and some thread, to cut her open and sew her back up. Certain traditions are sacred and the dying wishes of a folk-hero must never be opposed. All the same, she feels nervous at the thought of the impending funeral. She can't decide whether to hope for her own death, or not, before the actual burial. She is losing blood rapidly. The arrow still quivers in her womb. She reaches across for the jar and uncorks it with effort. The shape inside is whistling a dirge.

"Cut that out! The mourners will be here soon."

The Khazar god of dreaming chuckles. "That's right. How does it feel to be a grave? It's a nightmare scenario I wish I'd invented!"

"I don't intend to give you any work tips . . . "

"Haven't been able to send dreams to my people since you shut me up in here. You might as well let me go. Break the glass."

"No. I think you should be buried inside me with Robin, as a sacrifice."

"What? You can't mean that! I get claustrophobic enough as it is! Wombs are so dark and stuffy. Please don't!"

"What will you do for me if I spare you that fate?"

"I'll make you better, mistress! I promise!"

"You mean I'll get well again, even though this arrow is sticking in me? And I'll survive the funeral too? It's a deal."

"On condition that you release me afterward."

"I guess that's fair enough. Done!"

They don't shake hands on it. The little god casts his spell and is still cooling his fingers when the mourners enter the clearing, marching slowly with black armbands. Little John carries the corpse over one shoulder, Maid Marian wields the knife. Guy of Gisborne shudders when the first spurt of blood hits him in the eye. He hates solemn occasions.

•

The landlord of the *Damsel & Pointy Hat* has never known such a talkative group of revellers as the three strangers who are sitting in the corner, quaffing mead and roaring with laughter at each other's anecdotes. A lady with red hair, a scruffy giant with a bristling beard and a young blond man with blue eyes. Even when he was a carpenter, he never knew such rasping noises. They drink out of a Norman helmet, the nose-guard acting as a handle.

"And then I caught him wearing lingerie!" the blond one is shouting.

"Ho, ho, ho! Ha, ha, ha!" laugh the other two.

They are obviously holding a sort of farewell party for a deceased comrade. They don't seem to miss him too much. Perhaps he was overrated? Yes, that must be it.

"If only Robin was here to buy us all another round! He was a noble enemy. I almost wept tears when my sword sliced through his lungs."

The lady mutters into her drink. "Actually he was always a stingy old sod."

"Really? His reputation is quite the opposite."

"Yes, he kept the facts safely under lock and key. He was a bloody awful lover too. Very poor aim. Absolutely no stamina."

The giant grits his teeth. "Not sorry to see him go."

"Well this is a surprise," admits the blond fellow.

The door of the tavern swings open and a very tall woman staggers over the threshold. There is an arrow protruding from her midriff. She wears a pained expression.

"So this is where you got to? Charming, I'm sure, getting drunk while I have to lie on my back in the cold. Let me join you and make this a proper wake."

There is a spare seat. Nobody tries to remove it.

"Um, are you better then?"

"Indeed I am. Don't act so astonished. I'm the Queen of the Amazons and I know plenty of tricks to get out of a tight spot. First time I've had a whole man inserted inside me, though. It's a bit uncomfortable, but I won't complain. Tell me instead, where the heck did you get black armbands from in the forest?"

"Tore them in strips from Guy of Gisborne's surcoat."

"Liar! That item of fashion was red, not black."

"We stained it with berries."

"In February? I doubt it! Come on, be serious."

"We can't remember exactly. So there!"

"But little details like that are very important . . . Wait! I've got this terrible pain in my pelvic area! I'm having contractions! I'm about to give birth!"

"Quick! A towel and some hot water!"

"Too late! Here comes its head!"

"Ooh, what an ugly baby! Somebody give it a smack!"

Little John steps forward, his fingers bunched into fists.

"Wait! What's that it's saying as it plops fully out? It's trying to articulate its first sentence! A touching moment, this. Be silent and listen."

They lean closer, cupping their ears.

"Go take a Frying Tuck at the moon!"

Maid Marian rolls her eyes. "It's a boy! An overgrown, mansized boy!"

•

The Sheriff of Nottingham has reached the clearing in the forest. There are fifty mounted knights with him. They wear full armour and never speak, so it is difficult to be sure that anybody is inside. They are probably automatons, created by the wizard who lived in the castle before him. Certainly he found them all stacked neatly in the cellar. He recalls how he spent a whole afternoon cleaning the rust off with a little brush.

He reins his horse to a halt and sits creaking in the saddle. Beneath his own armour he can feel the tension of the stockings and suspender belt. They are wealing up his flesh nicely. And the black satin knickers are too tight. The year is 1193. Soon it will be the Thirteenth Century. He hopes his sex life improves in time.

"Look at that! An item of evidence!"

He points at the jar lying on the ground. It is empty now.

Some of his knights swivel their heads and snort gently. "Phasswass." That's the only sound they ever make. And "Shoowshss."

The Sheriff rubs his chin. "I recognise that vessel. I saw it in the possession of Nina, Queen of the Amazons, when she came to stay with me. She never showed me its contents, but they have gone now. Maybe alcohol. This puts me in mind of my own thirst. There's a tavern not far from here. If we gallop, we may reach it for a last one before closing time. And then we can resume our search for Guy of

Gisborne!"

"Phasswass . . . Shoowshss . . . "

"Yes, I miss him too. Onwards!"

•

Robin Hood is poking the tall woman with his finger. The firelight dances on his snarling face. A helmet of mead spills over as his leg knocks the edge of a table. There is shouting and many spluttered curses.

"So you think you're harder than me, do you, lady?"

For answer, she slaps him across the cheek and off his feet.

"In a word, yes," she spits at last.

He climbs to his knees, wiping the blood from his lips. "Play rough, eh? That's your game, is it? I may have been born after yesterday, but you won't gull me with another trick. Come on, lady, put them up."

"No trick!" she cries, as she slaps him with her other hand. "Just good honest violence. I've wrestled serpents in Lake Karatis."

Maid Marian, Little John and Guy of Gisborne are standing in a circle, clapping hands louder and louder. "Scrap! Scrap! Scrap!"

Robin Hood staggers upright a second time.

The landlord steps forward. "No brawling in the *Damsel & Pointy Hat*. This is a respectable establishment. Off the premises, the lot of you!"

"We'll settle this outside," snarls Robin.

Nina nods and turns to leave. As they all step through the door, Little John strokes his beard thoughtfully. "How come she gave birth to a live Robin Hood after they both died?"

"A bit confusing, isn't it?" agrees Guy of Gisborne.

Maid Marian shrugs. "Perhaps she had some magic potion that restored her to health and once Robin was buried inside her womb, the spell must have worked for him too, by accident. That must be what happened."

Little John and Guy of Gisborne gape. "Of course! It's so obvious!"

They are standing outside the tavern now. The Prince of Thieves is squaring up to the Queen of the Amazons. They circle each other warily.

"Look over there!" cries Robin suddenly. "It's a unicorn!"

She turns her head. "Where?"

And Robin rushes in and delivers two mighty punches to the side of her jaw. She staggers back and he chortles. "The oldest trick in the book!"

She glowers at him. Her rage is enormous.

"I can play dirty too!" she booms. Twisting up her face, she reaches down and draws the arrow out of her abdomen. She holds it like a dagger. Then she rushes forward and stabs him straight through the heart.

He groans once and collapses in the dust.

"Robin Hood is dead a second time! I have won the duel!"

Maid Marian, Little John and Guy of Gisborne crouch over the prone body and mutter to themselves. "Oh dear! Oh dear! We don't mind that he's dead. But we have to bury him wherever the arrow lands. And this has generated a paradox. We must bury him *inside himself*. How the hell can we sort this one out?"

•

The Sheriff of Nottingham and his fifty knights reach the tavern just as the sun begins to set. So he assumes that the blood trickled around the entrance is a trick of the light. Then he notices the little funeral taking place in the shadows.

"Show some respect, lads! Take your helmets off!"

On second thoughts, he's glad they can't.

He decides it's his moral duty to ride closer and exchange some pleasantries with the mourners. After all, this is his fiefdom and these people are his children, in a metaphorical sense. He is amazed when he discovers who they are.

"Guy of Gisborne! You traitor! You've joined my enemies!"

The blond head shakes emphatically. "Not at all. But the laws of chivalry compel me to assist in the burial of Robin Hood, even though the task is impossible."

The Sheriff dismounts. "Fair enough! But what's the problem?"

Guy of Gisborne waves a hand at the body, over which Maid Marian and Little John squat, exchanging ideas, all of them futile.

"We have to bury him inside himself and we're not sure how best to accomplish this. My view is that we ought to slit him open from throat to groin and fold his limbs into the gash and then apply enormous pressure on them until he turns inside-out. That's the only way I can think of discharging his final request."

The Sheriff's eyes twinkle. "Oh, impetuous Guy! How I love thee!"

"You think my idea has much merit?"

"Not at all! But it was presented to me in a charming tone. That's why I feel affection toward you. A big silly rascal, that's what you are! Listen, if I remember the conventions of chivalry properly, and I studied them when I was younger, the standard wording of such requests includes the word under."

"What do you mean?" frowns Guy of Gisborne.

"It's not 'bury me where the arrow lands', but under where it lands!"

Guy of Gisborne turns to the other two. "Hey! Did he say under?"

Little John scratches his head. "Under? Yes, I believe he did."

Maid Marian pounds a fist into her palm. "Bugger! I forgot that! Damn it, there was no need to bury him inside Nina, Queen of the Amazons, after all. We should have just interred him at the spot directly below her feet."

"Well, it's not too late to bury him that way now."

They regard the corpse. Guy of Gisborne clarifies the point: "You mean we just dig at that exact spot and put him in the hole?"

"Yes, but a coffin would be more dignified. The landlord of this tavern used to be a carpenter. I'll order him to knock up a box right away."

He turns and strides into the tavern. Without him, his knights grow restless.

"Phasswass! Shoowshss! Now we can chat properly!"

•

Isaac II Angelos, Emperor of Byzantium, sits on his throne and plays with his toys. The Magnaura Palace is very large and cold at night. There are hidden springs and cogs and levers in most items of furniture. In front of him stands a bronze tree with many branches, each of which is covered with little gilt birds. They sing various songs with their delicate metallic throats. Gone are the days when everything was very shiny. The mechanical tree, and the roaring gilt lions at the foot of the throne, are tarnished now and overused, for they date from the reign of Theophilus, who lived in the middle of the Ninth Century.

Similarly, the throne is connected to the rear wall by a device which can lift it to the ceiling along a disguised groove. There are changes of clothing inside the hollow seat. The idea was originally to impress ambassadors and visiting dignitaries from the west. A diplomat would be carried into the presence of the Emperor by two eunuchs and then set down. He would be expected to prostrate himself thrice, throwing himself at full length on the floor. Each time he looked up after one of these prostrations, the Emperor would be in a different position on the wall and in a new set of robes. It would be mystifying.

But now the workings are worn and inefficient. The throne squeaks as it jerks toward the ceiling, threatening to throw its occupant off.

A real bird flaps into the Palace and lands on the bronze tree.

It is a pigeon. The Emperor reaches forward and removes the message from its leg. He unrolls the paper and arches an eyebrow.

"A letter from the Sheriff of Nottingham," he says.

His Vizier bows deeply. "You asked him to keep you informed of developments."

"Did I? So I did! Now let's see, what does it say? Ah! Apparently some fellow called Robin Hood was killed by an arrow and was laid inside a new coffin and the lid was about to be secured and nailed down when Nina, Queen of the Amazons, threw herself on his body. He was her son, she wailed, and therefore she had no choice but to love him, even though she had killed him. She kissed him on the lips. To everyone's horror, the corpse returned to life. It seems that Nina had kept a god in a jar and had promised to let it go if it granted her a wish. It did so, but she cheated on her side of the bargain. She released it from the jar, yes, but by swallowing it! She chewed it up and digested it! Anyway, the magic powers inside the god must have transferred themselves into her metabolism, allowing her kiss to be suffused with implausible restorative qualities! So she kissed him back to life! But the story doesn't have a happy ending. Do you know why?"

The Vizier shakes his head. "Sorry, no. I don't speak Latin. This is Byzantium, and my language is Greek. I didn't understand a word of that!"

"Nor I! It's just a mass of squiggles. It doesn't matter anyway, because it will be out of date now. The events it describes are in the past."

The Vizier licks his lips. "Can we have the pigeon for lunch?"

•

Maid Marian, Little John, Guy of Gisborne, the Sheriff of Nottingham and the Queen of the Amazons are patiently explaining to Robin Hood why he must be buried alive. He is lying in his coffin and only Nina's foot on his chest prevents him from getting out. She holds the lid in her hands. She smiles sweetly.

"If there was another way, you know I'd take it."

"Call yourself a mother?" squeals Robin. "I'm alive now!"

"Yes, that was an enjoyable magic kiss. But the rules are clear. A final request must be obeyed, and you asked to be buried under the spot where your arrow ended up. It stuck in your own heart. So now we have to bury you here. The fact that you are a living person is completely irrelevant."

"But I'll suffocate down there and be dead again!"

"So what are you complaining about? That sorts everything out."

"I thought you loved me!"

"I do. As a mother loves a son. But there comes a time when two people, whatever their relationship, have to let each other go."

"I don't want to be buried alive! I don't want to be buried alive!"

"Oh stop whingeing, you little pansy!"

Pressing him down firmly, she positions the lid on the coffin. Maid Marian and Little John hurry forward with hammer and nails. There is much banging. The screams of Robin Hood are muffled now. The coffin is sealed.

"Lower it into the grave!" cries the Sheriff of Nottingham.

The pit is six feet deep. The coffin fits perfectly at the bottom. The knights kick the loose soil back until the hole is filled. Guy of Gisborne leads his horse over it a few times, to stamp it flat. The screams are now very faint. Perhaps they are not really there. It could just be a thousand worms writhing.

"I hate these ceremonies," says the Sheriff of Nottingham.

"Well it's all over now," replies Nina.

"What will you do? All of you, I mean."

Little John and Maid Marian exchange glances.

"I'm going to retire to a convent."

"So am I! After a shave, that is. And an operation."

Guy of Gisborne barks: "My place is still by your side!"

"Phasswass! Shoowshss!"

"And you, my Queen? What are your plans?" the Sheriff adds.

Nina sighs and looks around. Then she shrugs. "I've done what I came to do. I think it's time to return to Scythia. But what about you?"

"Oh, I owe the Emperor of Byzantium a long letter."

•

The Sheriff of Nottingham and his knights decide to accompany Nina, Queen of the Amazons, out of Sherwood Forest. But before they reach its edge, she reins in her horse and sighs. Then she turns around.

"It's no good. There's a big problem."

"What do you mean by that?"

"I can't leave Robin down there. He's my son now and I carry him in my heart. And the way things have ended up, he has to be buried below himself. I mean, that's what we've just done. So to keep to the spirit of the request, and the way we have interpreted it, he ought to be buried below wherever I am."

"But you'll be constantly on the move now!"

"Yes. Pity there's no such thing as a portable grave!"

He frowns. "Perhaps there is! Follow me!"

The Sheriff of Nottingham spurs his horse back to the *Damsel & Pointy Hat*. The grave lies off to one side. He dismounts and enters the tavern. After a few minutes, he comes out and signals to Nina.

"The landlord's a carpenter, remember? I asked him if he could make some sort of device like a snowplough to attach to the front of the coffin. He said, yes."

"You mean I'll be able to drag the coffin under me wherever I go?"

"Yes, the plough will automatically shift the earth aside. The grave will remain a constant six feet under all the way back to Scythia."

"Taking it across the Channel might be difficult."

"You can hire out a ship with a hold packed with soil."

The knights have already disinterred the coffin. The knocking from inside is very feeble. The landlord emerges from the tavern with the prepared device. While he fits it, Nina decides to open the lid for a last look.

Robin Hood's face is contorted. There is much sweat on his brow.

"Thank God! I was on my last breath!"

"I haven't come to rescue you, silly! Just to tell you that we're about to start on a long journey. We're going home, my dear son."

"What? What? What?"

She answers the question by replacing the lid.

A rope is secured from the coffin to her hand before the soil is replaced. Now she can pull the grave along behind her. When the rope is taut, it carries the vibrations of Robin's frenzied knocking. When she holds it close to her ear, she can hear his screams and pleadings. It will provide entertainment on the voyage.

They leave Sherwood Forest by a different route. She crosses a dry riverbed. The Sheriff of Nottingham is behind her. Behind him are the fifty knights. While they are still crossing, a giant scorpion bears down on them. Shocking what the Crusaders brought back with them! A terrific fight begins. Many of the knights really are empty suits of armour after all.

It is none of her business. She keeps going.

BROTHERS OF PASSION
Michael Laimo

It had to be a place where they could be alone. Quiet, filled with shadow. A place where they could bond together in their brotherhood. Tonight, they had found that perfect place: a solitary patch densely ensconced by nature, echoes of birds long lost in their nighttime abodes, their chirps replaced by whispering insects taking command of the night. Gentle breezes embracing the branches of the trees around them, a million leaves promising a century's worth of secrets in their static-toned sway.

They were brothers, bound not by blood, but by passion, their very souls dedicated to right the wrong in society, to rid away the evil thriving here since the birth of their personal devil, Nathan Bedford Forrest, brought unto this earth in the year 1821. Darren Robinson and Albert Johnson, two men sharing colour of skin and a commitment to save their kind from hatred, hid in this perfect place where their prayers filled the cool dark air in restless anticipation for the rise of occasion.

In the not-too-far distance: a noise.

They hunkered low amidst the shadows, the gathering a mere hundred yards beyond the wooded perimeter, a horrifying mass of white hoods and robes emerging, blood red crosses marring the angry white cloth shrouding these fiends, every thread of fabric symbolising the bloodied hatred passing through their veins. Triangles of death they were, milling in the brashness of their very own personal space, webbing themselves together in a contemptuous mass defining and continuing the work of Forrest himself. In their narcissistic unity, horrid strength prevailed, their brotherhood not unlike that of the secreted Darren and Albert, albeit their mission, dissimilar to great means.

The occasion unfolded, these cloaked executioners assembling in a forbidding circle, hands joined in prayer for violent death of those unlike themselves, those unlike their own rosy-skinned freckled kin who had spent a century and a half patronising their fathers: the leaders to whom they accredited rightful possession to the customs of the southern fatherland beneath their feet, and the land falling well beyond into the mountains.

Darren and Albert shuddered uncontrollably at the outspoken supplications from the gathered tribe. In response, they made their personal vows, committing to each other that they would indeed fight—even if death need be—in their personal struggle to cease this evil against their own kind, to put an end to the hatred just as their own leader had, the great Reverend Martin Luther King.

In their sweaty concealment, they pulled their weapons, handguns, one apiece, checking sure that each had been properly loaded.

The prayer beyond the cloak of the trees grew in volume. The tension of the moment surged. The two men took aim.

Then, a great heart-striking whump!

The unanticipated blast consumed the field before them, silencing the wildlife. Tears of indignation struck Darren's eyes, fuelled by the smoke of the great cross now aflame at the centre of the gathering. Unified cries of hatred exploded from the Klan members, *Die niggers! Die niggers! Die niggers!* over and over and over, the chant spookily echoing the crackles of the villainously formed blaze.

Darren cowered back, motioning Albert with him; each man swathed in glistening perspiration. The flames roared on, Darren wondering silently how they, two black men ineptly armed with a single solitary weapon, could possibly take down a crazed mob numbering a hundred or more—an entire tribe built solely on the inducement of hatred for the very blood coursing through their very own veins.

Then suddenly, silence. The chanting ceased.

With great curiosity Darren and Albert stared determinedly

through a crack in the shrubbery. They shuddered at the encroaching scene, never in their wildest musings expecting to glimpse such a vision. Immense confusion set in, and instantly and unwittingly, they became witnesses to a miraculous yet daunting event.

Ceasing their invocations, the klan members kneeled low to the ground, heads bowed in prayer to their god, heretofore unseen, now eerily manifesting from the seething whorls of smoke spiralling crazily from the flames. The smoke rose up, thickening into a great moon-like apparition that hung lazily above the burning cross: a face forming, the nose thick and bulbous, the eyes strong and staring and clearly capable of sight, the mouth contorted not in pain but in anger, plumes of black smoke spewing from within.

A single klan member, the Grand Wizard, rose and stood stoically before the ghostly vision, arms spread in invocation. "We summon you on this evening, great leader, on the anniversary of your death, to aid us in ridding our rightful land of the filthy virus known as the black man. Please, dear god, you, the divine Nathan Bedford Forrest; help us to continue what you so bravely started many years ago. I beg of you to have mercy and give us, the white man . . . give us back our deserved land lest we go on suffering in allocation of a stake that is rightfully our own!"

His voice echoed through the dancing flames. In this terrifying silence, Darren could hear Albert's frightened breaths, a response forced solely by an unanticipated fear of the unexpected.

Clearly, their guns would be of no use now, against the otherworldly.

"Darren," Albert finally stammered, whispering. "N-Nathan Bedford Forrest, he founded the Ku Klux Klan. I-I've gazed hatefully at portraits of the man. That," he said, pointing, "is . . . is his ghost. I *recognise* him. Dear Lord, they've summoned his spirit from hell!" Utter dread had hold of Albert, causing his voice to rise. Darren grabbed him by his shoulders, attempting to quiet him, but the man shook uncontrollably, eyes bulging in panic. He dropped his gun, trying to rub the fear from his face. "It c-can't be, Darren. It can't be!"

"Shut up! Do you want to get us killed?"

Despite his own trepidation, and the hysteria seizing Albert, Darren continued to stare at the ghostly apparition of Nathan Bedford Forrest, utter disbelief keeping him rooted to the earth: thick black smoke swirling fantastically, the unearthly features dramatically clear-cut, black eyes lolling, nose wriggling, the mouth stretching wide with great offence.

To Darren and Albert—two black men sent by their own passion to fight this evil—it seemed that Nathan Bedford Forrest had rejoined forces with the very organisation he founded over a century ago. It seemed that all their hopes and prayers had been burned away at the cross, just like that.

Then, suddenly and unexplainably, Albert broke away from Darren's grasp, out from the cover of the woods and into the open field. He stood silently at the perimeter of the woods, and for a moment it seemed to Darren that the briefest of chances existed for him to retrieve his friend without being spotted. But then the hysterical Albert started screaming out loud, pacing toward the congregation, pointing accusingly as tears streamed down his face. "You! Killers! You'll all burn in hell along with your God-forsaken leader."

Darren stayed back, cursing Albert's foolishness. He gripped his weapon tightly, although he knew deep inside he would not be using it. So instead he stayed silent, watching Albert as he continued to condemn the klan, pointing and screaming, his sudden insanity undoubtedly granting himself the death they promised to concede to, should their struggles demand it. *Dear God*, Darren thought, *why would he suddenly behave this way? It's suicidal.* It gave them nothing of pride to take to the grave.

The klan members, every single God-damned one, turned and gazed at the stumbling black man, the eyes beneath the slits in their hoods evilly reflecting the orange glow of the fire. They surrounded Albert and captured him, dragging him into the congregation, his screams and flails useless against the numbers, and Darren could do nothing but tearfully witness a truly horrific act: his brother of passion being tied to the smouldering cross and set aflame.

He watched as Albert's skin melted away from his body. He listened to his tortured screams.

And he watched as a smile of satisfaction formed on the thickening apparition of the original founder of the Ku Klux Klan, Nathan Bedford Forrest.

•

In the months that followed, Darren returned to the perfect place every night, invoking prayers for his lost brother of passion with great hope that he had hopefully found a place in the heavens with God. With great exaltation, he performed this ritual every day for an entire year until the anniversary of the devil's death came around once again.

When Darren returned to the scene of the travesty, they were there. The hoods of death, assembled on another perfect night for celebration, clear skies, its partial moon swinging lazily like a cradle; casting smoothed beams upon the great rigid cross, erected steadfastly at the crux of the assemblage. Wind breathing, the leaves waved, enticing all nocturnal life to respond in chatter.

Unaccompanied, Darren concealed himself in his perfect place, his judgment opposing his desire to contest the enemy. Albert's shocking death created a sense of logic in him: a realisation that battling this Goliath alone would be unreasonable, unfathomable. This time only prayer would be able to create any expectation for a chance to wage battle against this beast, the power of the klan, and its ghostly leader.

Their prayer began.

A great foreboding remembrance seized Darren, the images of last year's horror playing itself out again, and suddenly he wished that his desire to return here tonight—all those three hundred and sixty four nights—had not been so burning, so torturing. Perhaps he should have remained at home instead, erasing all recollection of the fateful night Albert had succumbed to the grasp of evil. He should have turned his shoulder to retribution, even if indeed his efforts had safely relied on prayer. Perhaps then he could have continued living as a member of society—even if oppressed—suppressing his anger and accepting the horrifying event as simply another in a string of adversities he would be expected to succumb to as a man of colour.

But it had not turned out that way.

And now he hid, watching through a wedge of shrubs as Nathan Bedford Forrest again appeared before his followers, the smoke rising up from the burning cross, shapeshifting into the face of the evil leader. The head, the eyes, the nose and mouth, all conforming into a living, seemingly breathing, sentient being.

The Grand Wizard stood, his invocations that of pure hatred. "Dear God, Nathan Bedford Forrest, we give you our thanks for your coming. We beg of your power, your living breathing power, and plead with you to exercise your knowledge to aid us in our plight. Dear God, help us rid our land of the virus known as the black man!"

Darren shuddered as the ghostly image of Nathan Bedford Forrest began to contort, its features flowing like warm syrup. The fire beneath reddened and flared to a great height, nearly shrouding the apparition, sparks scattering like a fireworks display. A horrifying roar divided the night, the fire splashing into a multitude of tiny flames that burned away into the air, leaving behind a smouldering cross, its flames barely ignited.

The congregation scattered in sudden fear, and from the ashes rose another spectre, an entire body formed of dark smoke and ashes, standing ten feet tall. It floated skyward just above the dying vision of Nathan Bedford Forrest, its dark oscillating limbs grabbing hold of the founder's very existence and sending great waves of white light into it, burning the evil entity into oblivion. Unearthly screams erupted, from both creatures, and then the ghostly ash-golem peered in Darren's direction, its face a content visage of retribution.

Albert's face.

When the unearthly screams subsided, all that remained of Nathan Bedford Forrest was a wisp of stale smoke, its shape long lost to the hands of Albert Johnson, a man who promised to wage his own personal battle to death in a grave crusade to free his people from hatred.

Darren smiled, and the ghost of Albert smiled back. And then it exploded, sending a great storm of ashes over the congregation of klan members, turning them . . . black.

And as the hundred or more white supremacists stripped themselves of their robes, wiping their eyes and faces of the flaky ashes, Darren turned and ran home, away from the place that had turned out to be perfect after all.

AUTHORS AND ARTISTS

Geoffrey Maloney has had over 30 short stories published in small press magazines and anthologies in Australia, the US and the UK in the last ten years. He won an Aurealis award for "The World According to Kipling" for the best fantasy short story published in the year 2000. Until recently he lived in Queanbeyan, NSW where he edited the Canberra Speculative Fiction Guild's anthology *Nor of Human* which received several nominations in the 2001 Aurealis Awards. He now lives in Brisbane with his wife and three daughters and in his spare time re-reads his ageing collection of Philip K. Dick novels in search of inspiration. An anthology of Geoffrey's short stories, *Tales from the Crypto System*, is due out from Prime Books in the US later this year.

Darrell Pitt. "I first started writing science fiction, but I've decided that my heart is filled with horror, so that's where I'll be dwelling from now on.

I have stories appearing in upcoming issues of *Potato Monkey* (Australia), *Burning Sky* (USA) and the *Hour of Pain* anthology (also USA).

Recently, I took out first prize in the Katherine Susannah Pritchard Writers Foundation award with my horror/suspense piece "Calculations".

Apart from that, I'm 36 and have a wife, a daughter and a pet rock named Herman."

Gene O'Neill lives and writes in the Napa Valley with his wife Kay, a substitute primary grade teacher at St. Helena Elementary School.

They have been married for thirty-six years, their grown children, Gavin and Kay Dee, living in San Francisco and NYC.

After surviving the Clarion Workshop in writing in 1979 Gene has seen over 80 of his stories published. Several of his stories have garnered Nebula and Stoker recommendations.

Gene writes full time now, recently finishing two novels—*The Burden of Indigo* and *Shadow of the Dark Angel*—which will be published by Prime Books in 2002. Upcoming in 2002 are original stories in *Redsine* and in the anthologies *Darkness Rising*, *RAW*, *Decadence*, and *Dead Cats Bouncing*. His collection of eight stories with an introduction by Kim Stanley Robinson and an afterword by Scott Edelman, *Ghost, Spirits, Computers & World Machines* is available in tpb by Prime Books. He appeared as the featured author in November 2001 on *Twilight Tales* website and during the 1st Quarter 2002 at *Dark Fluidity.com*. He is currently working on a third novel, *Deathflash*.

Chris McMahon graduated from the University of Queensland with an honours degree in Chemical Engineering in 1986 and currently works in Climate Change research. Chris has a lovely wife and two young boys, Aedan and Declan; and enjoys martial arts, movies, music and walking in the twilight.

Chris has completed four novels to date; *The Calvanni* (Fantasy); *Scytheman* (Fantasy); *The Starburst* (SF) and his latest book *Warriors of the Blessed Realm*—a Fantasy/SF action hybrid.

Chris's SF short story "The Buggy Plague", is to appear in *Orb Speculative Fiction*. Previous credits include the SF short stories "Old Man Saltbush" (*Redsine*) and "The Kite Flyers" (*alienq*).

Adam Browne lives in Melbourne with his wife, Julie Turner, also a writer. He has had numerous stories published online and in Australian magazines. His story "The Weatherboard Spaceship" has been shortlisted for this year's Aurealis award for best short sf.

Mark McLaughlin's fiction, poetry, artwork and nonfiction have appeared/are forthcoming in more than 375 magazines, anthologies and websites.

These include *Galaxy, Best Of The Rest 2, The Best Of Palace Corbie, The Best Of Enigmatic Tales, The Best Of HorrorFind, Bending The Landscape,*

The Last Continent: New Tales Of Zothique, and *The Year's Best Horror Stories* (DAW Books). He is the author of the story collections, ZOM BEE MOO VEE & Other Freaky Shows and Shoggoth Cacciatore And Other Eldritch Entrees. Also, he is the editor of *The Urbanite: Surreal & Lively & Bizarre*.

Michael Kaufmann is currently marketing his first novel, a near-future political/military thriller. Michael and Mark have collaborated before. Previously, they have sold stories to *Here and Now*, *The Black Gate*, *Darkness Rising*, and the *Weird Trails* anthology of strange Western stories.

By day, **David McAlinden** works hard at being a Municipal Tree Officer in Cheltenham. By night, he drinks red wine and expensive single malt whisky while writing stories on his sexy iMac. Occasionally, he will submit a food shopping list to publishers specialising in the postmodern short story.

Born in the mid 1960s, he has been writing short stories for a long time, and is presently working on his first novel, which will be violent, amusing and probably quite weird. "The Wrong Stuff" is (possibly) his first published story.

His favourite hobby is sneering.

Alison L. R. Davies is a writer of contemporary horror/dark fantasy from Nottingham in the U.K. Over the last year she has had stories published in magazines in the U.K, America and Australia.

More recently her work has been accepted for *Darkness Rising* (the first edition anthology and also next Summer's edition), *Tourniquet Heart*, an anthology on release by Prime Books in the States, and *Dark Horizons* the BFS dark fantasy magazine. She has also had work showcased with *Terror-tales* and a number of web E-Zines. She is currently working hard on a collection of shorts which she hopes to get published some time soon.

Jack Fisher has over 150 different sales to various markets, including *Space & Time*, *Transversions*, *Black October*, *Dark Regions*, *Indigenous Fiction*, *Not One Of Us*, *Dreaming of Angels*. His most recent and prominent to date has been his short fiction sale to *Cemetery Dance* magazine. Jack served as editor for *Whispers & Shadows*, available from Prime Books and *Strangewood Tales*, available from Eraserhead Press. Jack edits the award-winning dark fantasy magazine, *Flesh & Blood*.

Jess Butcher resides in Mississippi USA with his wife and two sons. Butcher is the author of two genre manuscripts (*Bishop's Moon* and *Leo's Niche*) and more than one hundred short stories.

Rhys Hughes is the sort of fellow who always uses more words to write his sentences than are strictly necessary to do the job perfectly well.

Michael Laimo's first novel *Atmosphere* is forthcoming in paperback in September 2002 from Leisure Books. He's published two collections, both in hardcover, *Dregs Of Society*, from Prime Books, and *Demons, Freaks, and Other Abnormalities*, with Delirium Books. As well, he's had two chapbooks published, *Within the Darkness, Golden Eyes* from Flesh and Blood Press, and *The Twilight Garden* from Miranda-Jahya. His work can be found in many anthologies and magazines, including *Dark Whispers, The Edge, Delirium Magazine, Unnatural Selection, The Best Of Horrorfind, The Dead Inn, Whispers and Shadows, The Book Of All Flesh*, and many others. He serves as associate editor for *Space & Time Magazine*, and fiction editor for *Bloodtype*, a hardcore horror anthology from Lone Wolf Publications. His website is at www.laimo.com. E-mail: Michael@Laimo.com.

Geoff Priest lives in Texas. His artwork can be found on a number of book covers from Cosmos Books and Prime. Visit his online gallery at www.briareos.com.

Mark Roberts writes, illustrates and designs in a variety of media. His contact details can be found at www.chimeric.co.uk.

LEVIATHAN 3
Libri quosdam ad scientiam, alios ad insaniam deduxere

Edited by Forrest Aguirre & Jeff VanderMeer

Leviathan Three is the third volume in the World Fantasy Award and British Fantasy Award finalist Ministry of Whimsy's Leviathan series. Twenty-seven beautifully surreal stories, informed by the exotic, yet infused with clear, controlled prose, give even the most voracious reader of the sublime an abundant feast of words and images. The tales are, by turns, experimental, traditional, uplifting, and mischievous. From the early decadent works of Gautier and Gourmont to experimental fictions by such established writers as Rikki Ducornet, Brian Evenson, Carol Emshwiller, and Michael Moorcock, to fresh perspectives from up-and-coming writers James Bassett, Brendan Connell, and Michael Cisco, Leviathan 3 fullfills the expectations created by prior volumes, while further exploring the expanse of convulsive beauty. Zoran Zivkovic's "Library" story suite, or short novel, provides the impetus and frame for the anthology, as each Library story is followed by a series of thematically similar selections. Zivkovic, a highly-respected Yugoslavian writer, has reached new heights of metafiction, intellectual play, and emotional resonance with these stories about books.

"*Perhaps the outstanding original anthology of 2002 . . . what the anthology promises it delivers, and story after story is intriguing reading.*" —**Locus**

Praise for previous volumes in the Leviathan series:

"*A big, handsome devil . . . just about everything wins reader confidence early and then maintains it with intelligent development*" —**Literary Magazine Review**

" *. . . One of the best collections of quality fiction at any level that I've seen in years.*" —**Tangent**

ISBN: 1-894815-42-4
Price: $21.95

WWW.MINISTRYOFWHIMSY.COM

Peep Show #2

Front-cover colour image by DAVID HO

Fiction by
DAVID J. SCHOW
RONALD DAMIEN MALFI
JAMES McCONNON
MEHITOBEL WILSON
SIMON LOGAN
ROBERT BUCKLEY
DAVID COWDALL
ALEX SEVERIN
BEV VINCENT
HORNS
CHRISTOPHER FULBRIGHT

Interior story illustrations by LUKE BRENNR

Magazine Specs: Colour cover, 5" x 8" trade paperback, 118 pages, perfect bound. ISSN 1473-3714

Price including postage:

$8 US, £4.50 UK, £5.00 Europe, £5.50 RoW

Please make all checks/cheques/postal orders and IMOs payable to PAUL FRY and send them along to:

Paul Fry, 15 North Roundhay, Stechford, Birmingham, B33 9PE, England

Or buy online with your credit card at:

Peep Show web site: http://peepshowmagazine.co.uk
Project Pulp: http://www.blindside.net/smallpress/read/Absolutes/PeepShow/
Firstwriter.com: http://www.firstwriter.com/store/magazines/peepshow.htm

peepshowmagazine.co.uk

short, scary tales publications

"Beautifully written, virtually hallucinatory work . . . connoisseurs of the finest in postmodern fantasy will find it enormously rewarding." —STARRED REVIEW, Publisher's Weekly

CITY OF SAINTS & MADMEN:
THE BOOK OF AMBERGRIS
Jeff VanderMeer

Introduction by Michael Moorcock

The collection that China Mieville called "one of the best books of 2001"—enhanced with 55,000 words of new material and innovative artwork and design by seven artists and three designers. **A sumptuous feast of text and illustration.** This collection contains VanderMeer's Theodore Sturgeon Award finalist novella "Dradin, In Love" and his World Fantasy Award winning novella "Transformation of Martin Lake".

" . . . *a masterful novel . . . complex and textured, decadent and decaying . . . a beautiful work of art, both as physical object and text.*"
—*Locus Online, 2002*

"*The hardcover edition of Jeff VanderMeer's CITY OF SAINTS AND MADMEN is an invitation to wonder, a portal to a mind altering experience, a catalyst for the imagination, a narrative, whose intricate complexity clarifies instead of confuses, a fantasy that informs reality. I can't think of any other recent book I am so certain will become a classic.*"
—*World Fantasy Award Winner Jeffrey Ford, author of The Portrait of Mrs. Charbuque.*

ISBN: 0-9668968-8-2
Price: $40.00
Published by: Prime Books (www.primebooks.net)

Printed in the United States
4886